Political Profiles
Michael Bloomberg

Michael Bloomberg

Political Profiles
Michael Bloomberg

Sandra H. Shichtman

Greensboro, North Carolina

Political Profiles

Joe Biden
Michael Bloomberg
Hillary Clinton
Al Gore
Ted Kennedy
John Lewis
John McCain
Barack Obama
Sarah Palin
Nancy Pelosi
Arnold Schwarzenegger

Political Profiles: Michael Bloomberg
Copyright © 2011 by Morgan Reynolds Publishing

All rights reserved.
This book, or parts thereof, may not be reproduced in any form except by written consent of the publisher. For more information write:
Morgan Reynolds Publishing, Inc., 620 South Elm Street, Suite 387
Greensboro, North Carolina 27406 USA

Library of Congress Cataloging-in-Publication Data

Shichtman, Sandra H.
  Michael Bloomberg / by Sandra Shichtman.
  p. cm. -- (Political profiles)
  Includes bibliographical references and index.
  ISBN 978-1-59935-135-3 (alk. paper)
  1. Bloomberg, Michael--Juvenile literature. 2. Mayors--New York (State)--New York--Biography--Juvenile literature. 3. Businesspeople--United States--Biography--Juvenile literature. 4. New York
(N.Y.)--Politics and government--1951---Juvenile literature. I. Title.
  F128.57.B56S457 2010
  974.7'043092--dc22
  [B]
                                                    2009054286

Printed in the United States of America
First Edition

To Sean Gaffey, my sincere thanks for your patience while explaining financial terminology
and
To Katie Appel, my sincere thanks for your patience in getting answers to my questions

Mayor Bloomberg attends the 2009 New York City Police Department Memorial Ceremony.

Contents

Chapter One
"Just a Regular Kid" 11

Chapter Two
Off to Graduate School 21

Chapter Three
Working on Wall Street 27

Chapter Four
Going It Alone 43

Chapter Five
Growing the Company 53

Chapter Six
Entering Public Service 65

Chapter Seven
Second Term Mayor 77

Chapter Eight
Defying Tradition 89

Timeline 100

Sources 102

Bibliography 108

Web sites 109

Index 110

A young Michael Bloomberg

Chapter 1

"Just a Regular Kid"

In the 1970s, Michael Bloomberg was a rising star at Salomon Brothers, a company that bought and sold stocks and bonds for its clients. He had taken the job at Salomon straight out of Harvard and had worked his way up to partner, learning all he could about the financial industry.

Somewhere along the way he had made an enemy, though, and found himself sidelined by the company he loved. He was "demoted" to the information systems department. "I had stirred the pot, lost the battle, and was paying the price," he said.

The demotion turned out to be one of the best things to ever happen to Bloomberg. It set him on a new path, one that eventually wound its way to a second career in politics and the office of the mayor of New York City.

Michael Rubens Bloomberg was born on Valentine's Day in 1942 in Boston—the only son of William Henry and Charlotte Rubens Bloomberg. A sister, Marjorie, was born in September 1944.

William Bloomberg was a bookkeeper for National Dairy (later Breakstone's), and he spent many hours each day at his job. Charlotte—Lottie to her family—was a homemaker "of liberal views and independent mind." She had graduated from New York University in 1929 and worked as an assistant auditor in the New York office of National Dairy. Her boss introduced her to William Bloomberg.

The couple married in 1934, and they lived in the Allston neighborhood of Boston until Michael was two years old. Next they moved to Brookline, another Boston suburb, and rented a home. Then they decided to buy their own home in Medford, Massachusetts, which was closer to the dairy's offices.

Medford has long had its own niche in American history. Paul Revere famously galloped through Medford in 1775, during the American Revolution, warning of the coming British. In 1852, Universalists founded Tufts College there. Set on Walnut Hill, the highest point in Medford, Tufts was established as a "light on the hill."

In its early days, Medford also developed a reputation for its thriving tradition of ship building and rum production. But by the time the Bloombergs decided to move there, Medford was a blue-collar city, home to mostly Irish and Italian families. Not too far from Boston, the suburban city featured a conventional Main Street, with Brigham's Ice Cream Parlor, a funeral home, a library, two movie theaters, and an armory.

"Just a Regular Kid"

Charlotte Bloomberg chose the perfect stone-and-clapboard house for her family—a two-story with three bedrooms, a finished basement, and an attic. But there was one problem: the seller refused to sell to Jews. William Boomberg was the son of a Russian Jewish immigrant; Charlotte's father was also a Russian Jewish immigrant, born in present-day Belarus.

The Bloombergs found a way around the anti-Semitism, however. "Our lawyer, George McLaughlin, who was Irish, bought the house and sold it to us," said Charlotte Bloomberg. And, once the family settled into the house, she said everything was fine: "Nobody on the street was unpleasant to us."

William and Charlotte taught their children the value of hard work, civic responsibility, setting goals for themselves, and striving to achieve their goals. Michael later recalled that his parents taught him "to strive relentlessly."

Growing up, Michael was "just a regular kid," his mother said. He liked snakes, which he'd find among trees near the family home, and he'd use them to scare his younger sister. But he also had a serious side. A mentally disabled aunt lived in a nearby town and often needed help. Michael never failed to provide that helping hand.

Michael attended public schools in Medford—Gleason Elementary, Hobbs Junior High, and Medford High. He was neither a straight-A student nor a great athlete, and he got into his fair share of trouble. "I had discipline problems," Bloomberg acknowledges. "I threw erasers. I dipped pigtails into inkwells—I was totally bored."

But he was competitive and driven and liked to take charge. "Anything that came along, he wanted to do it," his mother recalled. "He wanted to be the boss of whatever we were working on. He wanted to run everything."

Political Profiles: **Michael Bloomberg**

During the 1950s, Michael joined the Boy Scouts of America. He loved working for merit badges and rising in the ranks, so much so that while preparing for his bar mitzvah, he sold Christmas wreaths door to door to pay for Boy Scout camp.

Bloomberg with his parents and sister

He became an Eagle Scout quickly, one of the the youngest in the Scouts' history to achieve that rank.

Every year, to commemorate the ride Paul Revere made on the night of April 18, 1775, a man dressed as Revere rides his horse through Medford's streets as part of a parade. When Michael Bloomberg was a boy, the parade ended at Winthrop Square, where a Boy Scout recited William Wordsworth Longfellow's poem, *Paul Revere's Ride.*

"Perhaps the proudest moment of my early life was being chosen one year to read [Longfellow's poem] on the raised platform overlooking the assembled revelers," Bloomberg later recalled. "With 'Paul' on his prancing horse in front of me, the high school band playing John Philip Sousa marches, and newspaper photographers snapping away, I read aloud into a real live microphone the famous poem: 'Listen, my children, and you shall hear/Of the midnight ride of Paul Revere./On the eighteenth of April, in Seventy-five. . . . '"

In addition to his regular school work, Charlotte Bloomberg arranged for her son to receive instruction in Hebrew studies. He first attended a shul in a house in Medford, but Charlotte later transferred him to a more established synagogue in Brookline.

Michael graduated from high school on June 3, 1960. His grades were unremarkable—he earned a D and three Cs in college preparatory math during his senior year—but he was president of the Slide Rule Club and a member of the Debate Club, enough to get him into Johns Hopkins University in Baltimore, Maryland, to study electrical engineering.

At Johns Hopkins, he paid his tuition with a government loan and worked at the faculty club parking lot, where he attended cars for dinner and earned $35 a week. Somehow, after paying his expenses, he found enough money to contribute to charities.

Bloomberg becoming an Eagle Scout in 1955

Political Profiles: **Michael Bloomberg**

A roommate once spotted a check written to the National Association of Colored People (NAACP) on Bloomberg's desk. It was around the same time Duke Ellington had visited the campus but was denied access to one of Bloomberg's favorite establishments. When the roommate saw the check, he asked, "What the hell are you doing that for, Mike?"

According to the roommate, Bloomberg told him that "we all need to be treated the same way, that if something bad can happen to someone who is black, it can happen to someone because they are Jewish or whatever...."

Bloomberg got along well with his schoolmates, displaying traits that helped him with his social life. He became president of his fraternity, Phi Kappa Psi, president of the Inter-Fraternity Council, and president of his class. He graduated in

Harvard University

"Just a Regular Kid"

1964 with a bachelor of science degree in electrical engineering and thought about what he wanted to do next. He decided to apply to Harvard Business School.

When the acceptance letter arrived, Bloomberg was with friends. "Great. Got in. Let's go get a cup of coffee," he said, without opening the envelope. A friend asked, "Don't you want to open it?"

"What's the point?" said Bloomberg. "They're not sending me a thick package if it was a rejection. That comes in a very thin letter."

Chapter 2
Off to Graduate School

At Harvard, Bloomberg studied accounting, marketing, management, and finance. He learned how to analyze and solve problems and to explain how he arrived at those solutions. But, just as he had at Johns Hopkins, Bloomberg received average grades in his courses.

"In graduate school, you were supposed to write ten pages solving a problem, and I wrote half a page saying there really wasn't a problem because one of the facts was wrong," he later recalled. "After the second time I did that, I got called in and it was explained to me that if I wanted to graduate, then I'd stick

Bloomberg's high school yearbook photo, 1960

Political Profiles: **Michael Bloomberg**

to the rules, look at what they're trying to do, and don't be a cute wise guy."

During the summer between his first and second year at Harvard, Bloomberg worked for a real estate firm in Cambridge, Massachusetts. It was a company that rented apartments to college students. Bloomberg got to work at 6:30 each morning. Because he arrived at the office before the other agents did, he answered the phone when it rang and made appointments to show the apartments to the students who called. The other agents were surprised when students came into the office asking for "Mr. Bloomberg."

Bloomberg received his MBA in the spring of 1966, but he had no particular plans because he expected to get drafted.

At the time, the United States was involved in a conflict in Vietnam, a nation in Southeast Asia. Vietnam was a divided nation—communists controlled the North and anti-communists controlled the South. Fearing the spread of Asian communism,

Soldiers in combat during the Vietnam War

Off to Graduate School

Lyndon Johnson, thirty-sixth president of the United States

the U.S. started sending equipment, aid, and military advisors to the country, and in 1965, President Johnson ordered bombing raids on North Vietnam.

More than 1.4 million American men were drafted during the last half of the 1960s, and Bloomberg expected to be among the draftees. So he decided to enlist and get his military service out of the way before starting a career. But the draft board rejected him, classifying him 1-Y for flat feet. "I've always felt a little lacking, a little embarrassed, that I wasn't in the Army," Bloomberg said in later years.

A friend suggested that Bloomberg contact two New York securities companies, Salomon Brothers & Hutzler and Goldman, Sachs & Company. He was not familiar with either company.

"Who are they? What would I be doing?" he asked his friend. He learned that each job would require him to pick up the telephone and talk to customers in order to bring in business.

At Goldman Sachs, he interviewed for a position as a trader. Then he went to Salomon Brothers & Hutzler for an interview. At the time, Salomon Brothers was a small company. The personnel manager showed him around. Then he was interviewed by the sales manager and by John Gutfreund, a partner at Salomon

23

Brothers. The last person to interview Bloomberg was William R. Salomon, the managing partner of the company.

He received job offers from both companies. Goldman Sachs offered him a salary of $14,000 per year. Salomon Brothers offered him just $9,000 per year.

Bloomberg liked what he saw at Salomon Brothers, and he thought he'd feel more comfortable working there than at Goldman Sachs. But the salary they offered was considerably lower than what Goldman Sachs offered him. It was also lower than what someone with an MBA could expect to get. So Bloomberg decided to negotiate his salary.

"Look, I can't afford to work at Salomon," he told John Gutfreund. "I want to. I'd love it. But I don't own another suit of clothes. I don't have an apartment to live in. I have no cash in the bank. All I've got are outstanding National Defense loans I took for tuition [at Johns Hopkins] when my part-time campus job as a school parking-lot attendant didn't pay enough."

"How much do you need?" Gutfreund asked him.

Bloomberg said, "I need $11,500."

Gutfreund replied, "Fine. That's $9,000 salary and a $2,500 loan."

Bloomberg accepted the job offer and the loan. His career was about to begin.

Opposite page: Baker Library at Harvard Business School. William Bloomberg died a year before Michael Bloomberg went to Harvard, but he would have been proud of his son. "For Dad, an average working-class guy from Chelsea, Massachusetts, Harvard was a rarefied and almost unattainable waypoint on the trail to the great American Dream," said Michael Bloomberg.

Manhattan skyscrapers

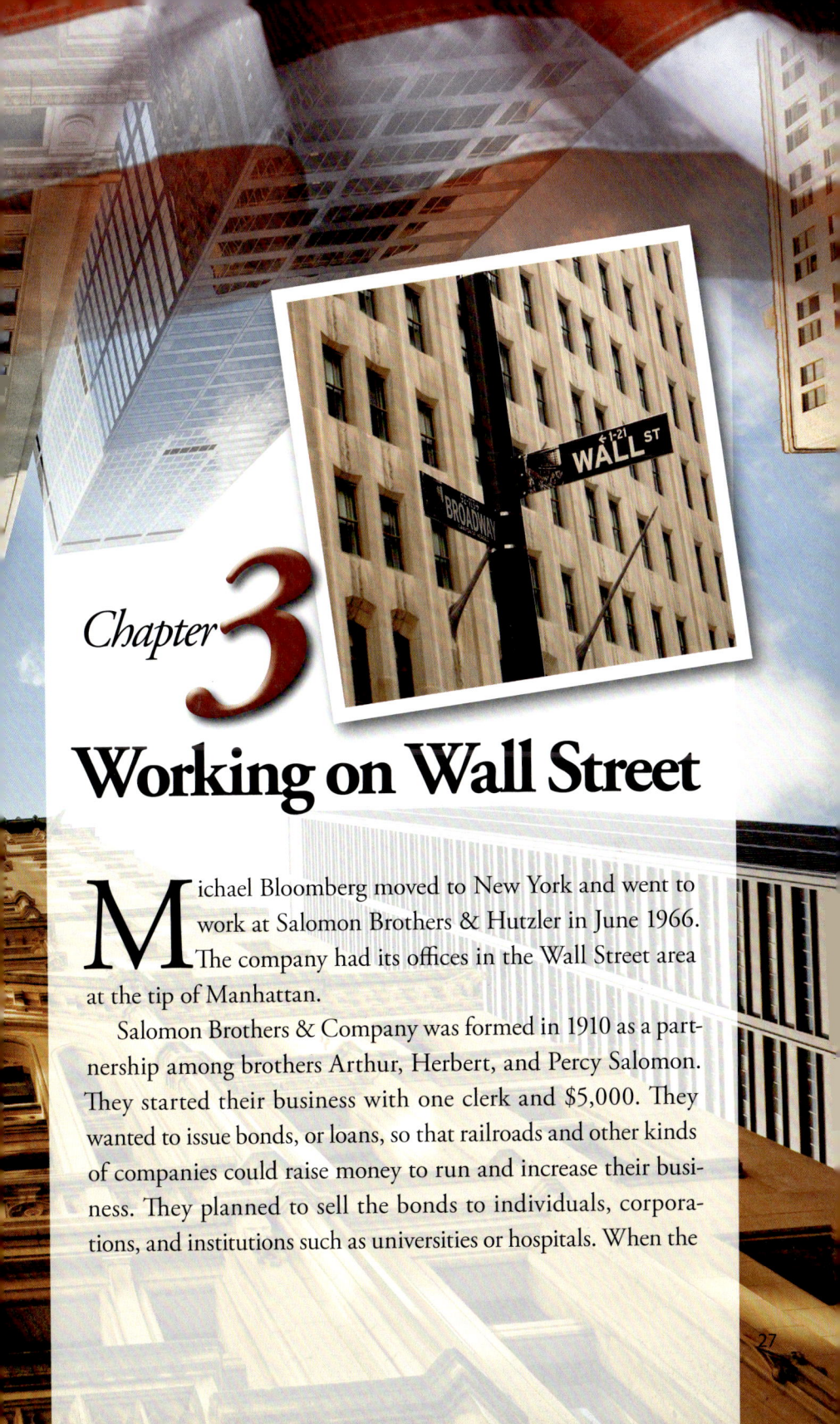

Chapter 3
Working on Wall Street

Michael Bloomberg moved to New York and went to work at Salomon Brothers & Hutzler in June 1966. The company had its offices in the Wall Street area at the tip of Manhattan.

Salomon Brothers & Company was formed in 1910 as a partnership among brothers Arthur, Herbert, and Percy Salomon. They started their business with one clerk and $5,000. They wanted to issue bonds, or loans, so that railroads and other kinds of companies could raise money to run and increase their business. They planned to sell the bonds to individuals, corporations, and institutions such as universities or hospitals. When the

 Political Profiles: **Michael Bloomb**

bonds "matured," the company that issued them would pay back the loans with interest. Salomon Brothers would make money, too, by taking part of the interest as a fee.

The brothers soon realized that they needed to have a seat on the New York Stock Exchange, so that they could buy and sell stocks as well as bonds. They could not afford to purchase a seat on the stock exchange themselves. So, a few months later, they merged their company with Morton Hutzler & Company, which had such a seat. The company changed its name to Salomon Brothers & Hutzler.

By 1966, when Michael Bloomberg was hired, Salomon Brothers & Hutzler had grown into a large company with hundreds of traders who bought and sold stocks and bonds for their customers. Many of the traders were partners in the company. When Bloomberg joined the firm, William R. Salomon was the managing partner, and he made all the most important decisions. He was the son of Percy Salomon, one of the founding brothers. Bloomberg once described the company as "a meritocracy that prized go-getters, tolerated eccentricities and treated both Ph.Ds and high school dropouts disinterestedly.

28

"I fit it," he said. "It was me."

Bloomberg's first job was to count the stock and bond certificates by hand. After the certificates were counted, messengers took them over to banks that were located in the Wall Street area. The certificates were used as collateral for overnight loans.

Any real object can be used as collateral. A person who wants to borrow money from a bank or another kind of financial institution might put up a home, a car, or jewelry as collateral. A company might put up its machinery as collateral to back a loan. If the borrower does not repay the loan, the bank keeps the object offered as collateral. Since stocks and bonds have real money value, their certificates can be used as collateral.

Banks use the money value of the certificates to conduct their business each day. They borrow the money value of the certificates so that they can have cash on hand for their customers and then pay it back with interest.

Political Profiles: **Michael Bloomberg**

When the banks returned the certificates from Salomon the next morning, they needed to be counted again to make certain none had been lost. Michael Bloomberg counted them again.

Salomon Brothers & Hutzler was a civic-minded company and required that their employees be concerned with helping others, too. Every employee was required to make a donation to charity. Since being civic-minded and charitable were things William and Charlotte Bloomberg had taught their children, Michael Bloomberg had no trouble continuing this tradition at work.

After he'd worked for the company for a year, Bloomberg was transferred to the trading floor at the New York Stock Exchange. He became a clerk at the utilities desk, where bonds of electric and gas companies were bought and sold. Two partners at Salomon Brothers ran the utilities desk, and Bloomberg's main job as the clerk was to keep the position book. A position book is an institution's record of the securities that it owns. The clerk tracks the trading of those positions, keeping the position book up-to-date as the bonds are bought and sold.

Bloomberg moved again soon after, this time to the equities desk, where it was his job to buy and sell stocks and bonds. He quickly learned that he was good at his job.

The New York Stock Exchange

Political Profiles: **Michael Bloomberg**

> *We could sell anything to anybody. We just did what all good salespeople do: We presented everything we had, and then highlighted whatever facts enabled customers to convince themselves they were getting a good deal. . . . I was the fair-haired boy, the block-trading superstar. I was the pet of its two top executives. I greeted all important visiting customers, got interviewed by every newspaper that mattered, and had a great social life playing the role of Wall Street power broker to the hilt. More than a 'legend in my own mind.'*

Bloomberg enjoyed working on Wall Street and the excitement of living in New York City. "I didn't love Wall Street just for the money, I also loved it for the lifestyle it provided," he said. By this time he was earning a good salary, which enabled him to eat at fine restaurants, and he had an expense account, through which Salomon Brothers paid for the meals and evenings out with clients.

As he had when he first came to New York, Bloomberg continued to travel to and from work on the subway. He got to work at 7 A.M., when no one but William Salomon was there. So, when Salomon needed someone to talk to, he talked to the only other person in the office—Michael Bloomberg—and the two men became very friendly. Bloomberg also remained at his desk after everyone had gone home but John Gutfreund, who was always the last person to leave at night. If Gutfreund wanted someone to talk to or needed to have something done, he went to Bloomberg. The long hours Bloomberg spent at work soon paid off for him.

By September, Bloomberg was promoted to the purchase and sales department. Employees who worked in this department received and checked in bills and receipts, making certain that all of the company's bills were paid and that the money it received was properly recorded.

Bloomberg noticed that stacks of years-old newspapers, especially the *Wall Street Journal*, and notebooks were kept in the purchase and sales department. The newspapers told the traders what the prices of stocks and bonds of publicly traded companies were each day. The notebooks listed the names of customers and what stocks and bonds they bought and sold and at what price. Each time a customer bought or sold a stock or a bond, the trade had to be recorded in a notebook. The newspaper helped the trader figure out the price at which it was traded. The trouble was that it took a great deal of time for each trader to do this work because it had to be done by hand.

Bloomberg knew that computers were beginning to be used to store information. He thought that Salomon Brothers's traders would benefit from having all their data or information stored in a big computer, called a mainframe, and then accessing or getting the specific information they needed from a computer terminal on their desks.

So he talked to John Gutfreund and William Salomon about computerizing the data. "I'm told it won't take long or cost very much," he told them. "We'll get instant access to the data we collect manually in all those books and even to those 'inaccessible' records stored on the company's mainframe computer." The inaccessible records were the ones that traders could not find.

Gutfreund and Salomon thought it was a good idea and told Bloomberg to go ahead and look into it. Bloomberg spoke to people he thought could best help him and convinced them that a computer terminal on the desk of each trader would be good for

Political Profiles: **Michael Bloomberg**

the company. The next step was to bring the idea to the executives at Salomon Brothers who would make the final decision.

The executives agreed that Bloomberg should continue to investigate putting a computer terminal on every trader's desk. "But you can only work on it part-time so it doesn't get in the way of your main responsibilities, selling equities," they said.

Bloomberg agreed to work on the project on his own time. He worked with a computer programmer who was also willing to work on the project after his regular job was finished, without getting paid extra money for it. In 1970, Bloomberg and his programmer began to put together an online information system.

One of their greatest challenges was to make certain the terminals were easy to use by traders who did not know much about computers. The terminals also had to be useful to Salomon Brothers employees who were not traders and to those who worked in its offices outside the United States. Before long, Bloomberg and his programmer had computerized all of the information, allowing Salomon Brothers's traders to quickly find the information they needed. Now, they no longer had to search through mountains of newspapers and notebooks to find it.

Each year, Salomon Brothers published a list of the new general partners. In 1972, Bloomberg expected to see his name on the list. After all, he had produced a computerized program that enabled Salomon Brothers's traders to be more productive. When he saw that his name wasn't on the list, he became angry. "I'll quit," he said to himself. "I'll kill 'em. I'll shoot myself."

Instead, he said nothing. To his surprise, later that year and without warning, he

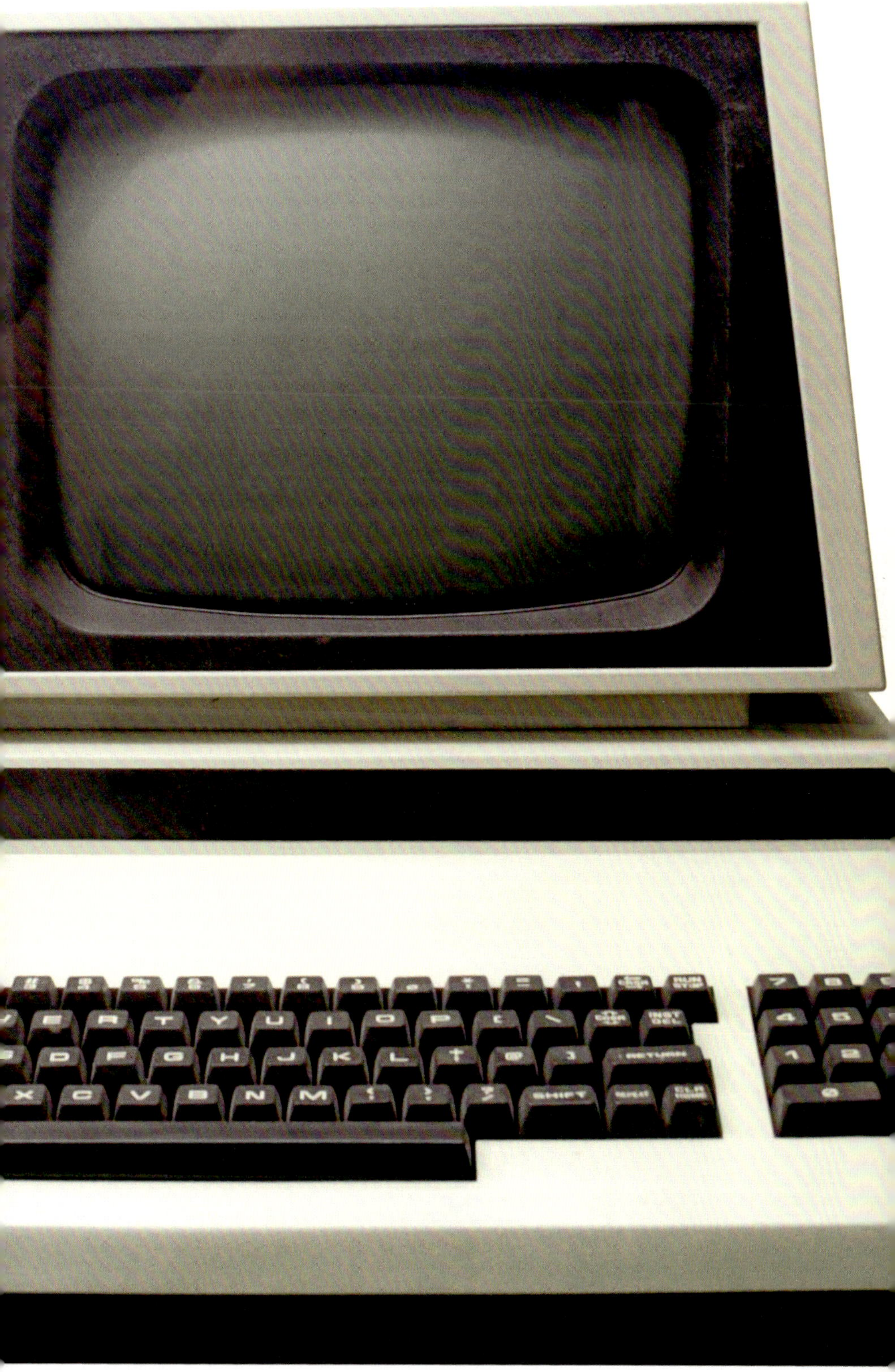
RETURN
SHIFT

Michael Bloomberg has always set high standards for himself. "I remember him telling me that it was very important to be successful," a high school friend recalled, "[and] that he was going to be successful because once you had a lot of money you could do things to improve the world."

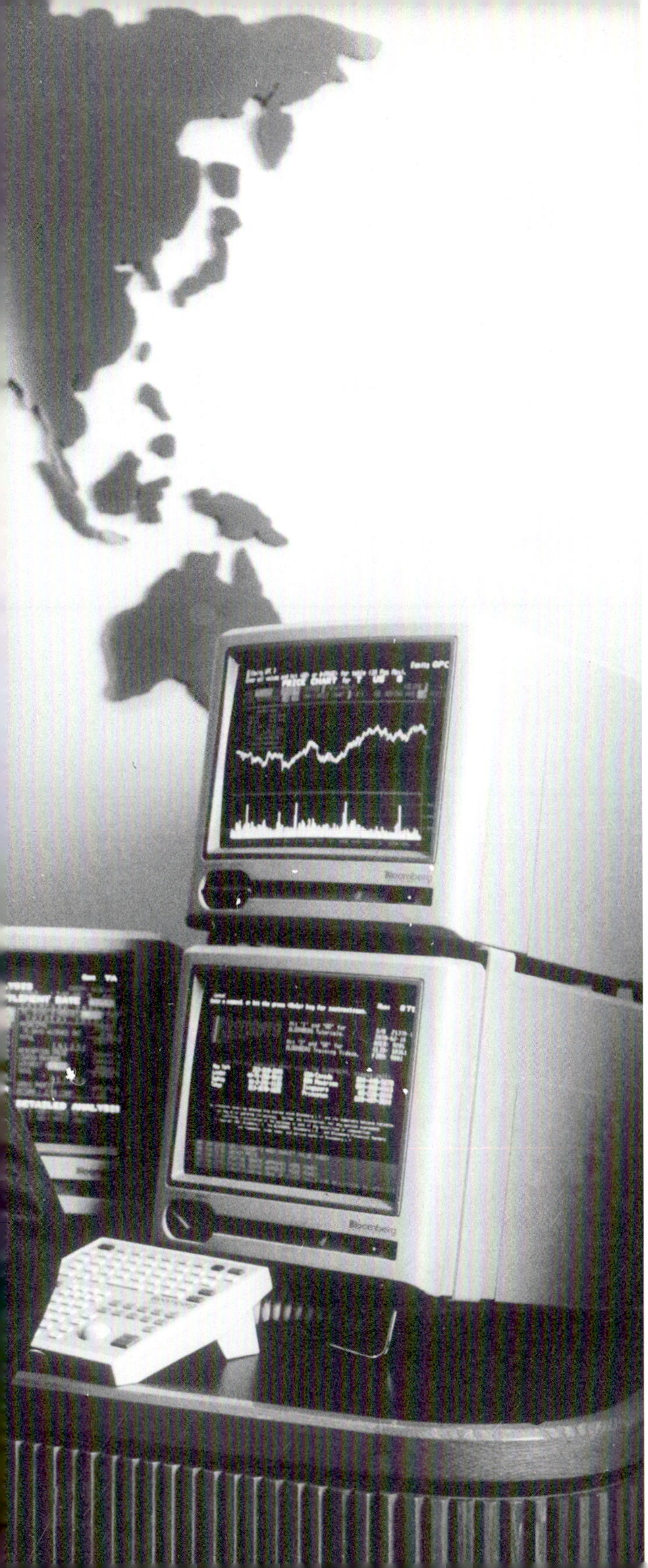
PRICE CHART
Bloomberg
Bloomberg

Political Profiles: Michael Bloomberg

learned that he was being made a general partner. As a general partner, he would be responsible for supervising the equities department, where traders bought and sold stocks and bonds for their customers. He would also be responsible for the arbitrage department, where customers made small profits buying or selling stocks and bonds based on probabilities, such as the issuing company buying, selling, or merging with another company.

His boss, Jay Perry, had run the equities department. But, as the result of an argument Perry had with Richard "Dick" Rosenthal, the head of the arbitrage department, both he and Rosenthal were transferred and their departments needed new leaders. So, the firm combined the two departments and gave Bloomberg the job of running them.

During the 1970s, Bloomberg also learned to fly a helicopter and earned his license to fly one. One day, while he was flying a rented helicopter over Long Island Sound, he heard a loud noise and saw smoke coming out of the engine. He didn't have to think about how to react in an emergency. "That's what all the training's for," he told a reporter years later. "You can't look for the switch, you have to know where it is." He landed safely. He also became the owner of his own helicopter.

In 1975, Bloomberg married Susan Brown, a native of Yorkshire, England. Susan had worked as a secretary in Salomon's London office, and had settled in New York after a divorce. "I think I remember we met on a hot dog line one lunchtime," said Susan, who had worked as a temp one day at Salomon Brothers. "Michael was pushing his way to the front and he rather annoyed me. I think I put my foot out." Bloomberg, then thirty-four, and Susan, twenty-eight, married in the study of Rabbi David Posner. The couple had their first child, a daughter who they named Emma, four years later in 1979.

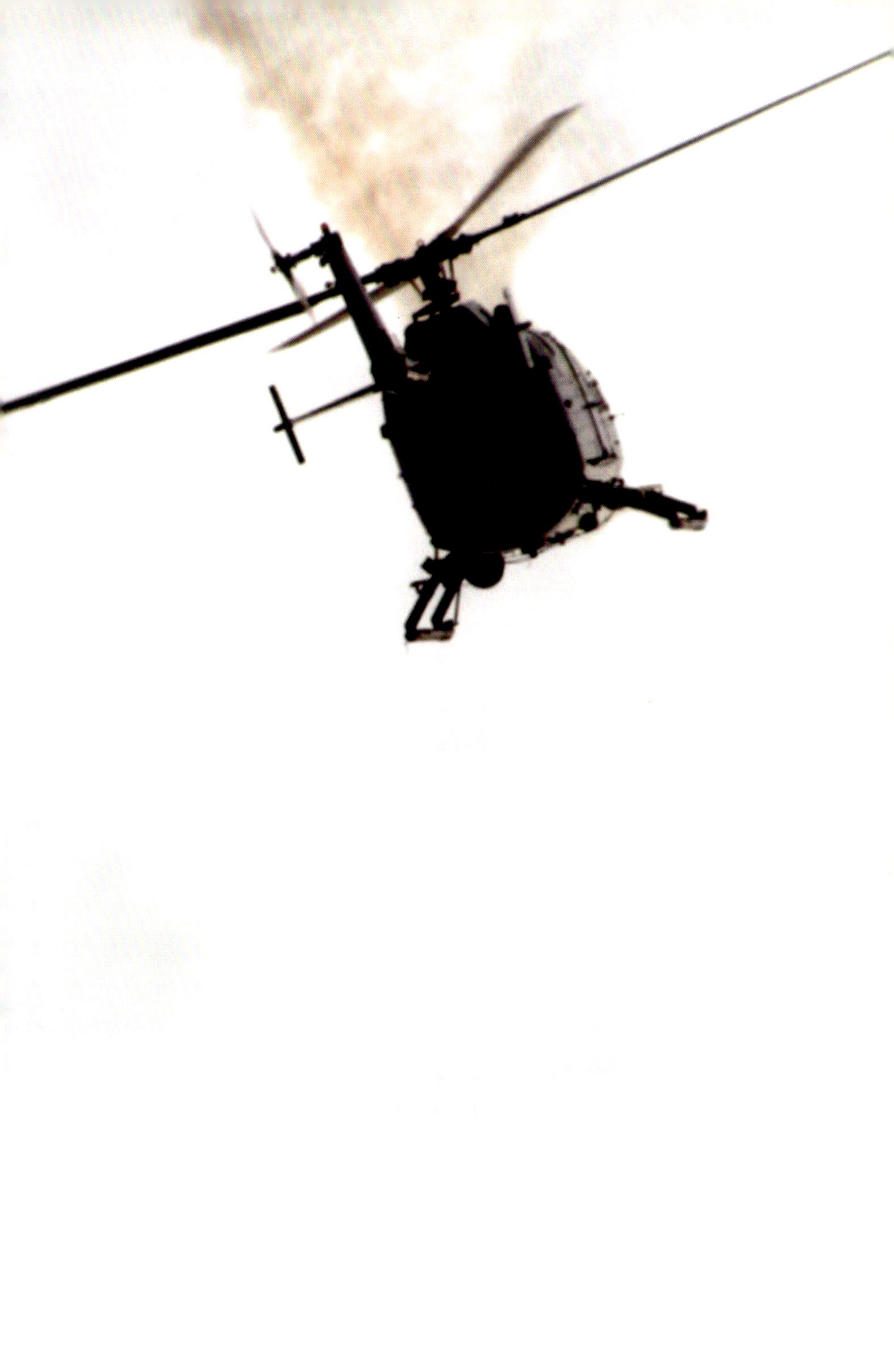

Political Profiles: **Michael Bloomberg**

By the late 1970s computers were being used by companies throughout Wall Street. Bloomberg was transferred to Salomon's Information Systems area, where he was asked to oversee the company's computer system. Because Bloomberg was seen as Jay Perry's "boy" and Perry had fallen out of favor at Salomon Brothers because of his argument with Dick Rosenthal, Bloomberg's star had stopped rising. He was pushed to the sidelines with this job. "He got put on a floor all by himself, the forty-fourth floor, I think," said a co-worker of Bloomberg's. "A bunch of us kids would hang out with him on his floor. It was like a no-man's land." Although he did not know it at the time, this would be his last position at Salomon Brothers.

In August 1981, Bloomberg and a group of other Salomon Brothers employees were called to a conference in Tarrytown,

View of New York City from the "Top of the Rock" observation deck on Rockefeller Center

New York. They were told that the company had been sold to Philbro Corporation, and that they were being laid off.

"I got into the car for the twenty-five-minute drive back to Manhattan," Bloomberg remembered years later. "I think I was probably a little bit upset. Nobody likes being pushed out. But, you know, you can't feel sorry for yourself. . . ."

WALL ST
1-21

Chapter 4
Going It Alone

Michael Bloomberg had one month to go before he would leave Salomon Brothers. But he was not leaving empty-handed. Salomon Brothers gave him $10 million in severance.

Bloomberg spent the rest of his time there deciding what his next move would be. Would he look for another job on Wall Street? Would he not work at all? After all, $10 million was a lot of money and a person could live quite nicely for the rest of his life with that much in the bank. Or, should he use the money to start his own business?

Bloomberg decided to start a business that would combine the two things he had the most experience in—securities and computer technology. He thought about what the securities industry needed but no one had yet provided. That's when he came up with the idea of starting a business that would provide computerized information for bond traders similar to what he'd created for Salomon Brothers. His customers would be able to access information on a terminal that sat on their desks.

This new business would help people working in the banking, securities, and investment industries acquire the most up-to-date information. It would allow individuals within those companies to analyze that information and use it in their daily work. For example, it would help them let their clients know whether one bond would bring them a greater return on their investment than another would.

Bloomberg told his wife, Susan, about his idea to start a business. "It'll mean I'll have to work a lot harder than I've ever worked," he told her. "Are you okay with that?" Susan responded yes, but years later she would find that Bloomberg's commitment to the business often interfered with family life.

First, Bloomberg searched for an office for his business. He looked at various spaces that were available and, finally, rented one. On October 1, 1981, Michael Bloomberg became an entrepreneur, or small business owner. He called his new company Innovative Market Systems.

He hired three former Salomon Brothers employees to help him start his new business. He hired Duncan MacMillan to collect and put into the terminals the data each future customer would need and Chuck Zegar to create the software infrastructure for the new company. He hired Tom Secunda, who had moved on to work as a trader at Morgan Stanley, a financial services company, to design and program the service. Michael Bloomberg would be the salesman for the company. Bloomberg later described his company as "four guys, one room and a coffee pot."

Secunda began working at Innovative Market Systems in February 1982. "We all worked six days a week and half a day on Sundays. We were creating something completely new. It was so exciting that it didn't even feel like work. It was probably the most fun I've ever had in my professional life."

The people who work in most companies have titles, such as vice president, president, or chief executive officer. Bloomberg wanted his new company to be unique or different from the others. He decided that he and his employees would not have them. Everyone would have his or her own responsibilities, but not a title. "I've always thought titles are disruptive at best," Bloomberg said. "They separate, create class distinctions and inhibit communications." His company would be different in another way, too. He and his employees would work in a single open space, rather than in separate offices. Free snacks, hallway fish tanks, parties, and an insistence on company loyalty and nose-to-the-grindstone work ethic were other unique features of the Bloomberg corporate culture.

Bloomberg's first customer was Merrill Lynch. In December 1982, Merrill Lynch ordered twenty terminals and agreed to pay

Political Profiles: **Michael Bloomberg**

Innovative Market Systems $600,000 for developing and building them and $1,000 each month per terminal every year until the contract was finished.

Bloomberg thought about how much money the contract would bring into his company, "I remember writing 20 x $1,000 on the back of an envelope thinking, 'That would cover our overhead,'" he recalled years later. "Today, it wouldn't cover our food bill." Michael Bloomberg had made the sale. But he'd sold a product that didn't exist yet.

Merrill Lynch assigned two of its traders to work with Innovative Market Systems. They knew the specific information Merrill would need to have them put into the terminals. Together with Bloomberg's people, they began to build the first terminal and the software to run it.

They worked feverishly to get the job done. Tensions ran high. Sometimes, when they faced difficult problems, Bloomberg would shout, "We're out of control! We're going to be out of business if this continues!" But they continued to work, solving the problems as they arose. By late 1982, twenty terminals, keyboards, and monitors had been installed at Merrill Lynch.

Merrill Lynch was satisfied that Bloomberg had lived up to his promise. He had delivered all twenty terminals on time. Merrill Lynch liked them so much that they signed Innovative Market Systems to a deal in which Bloomberg was forbidden to sell his terminals to any of Merrill's competitors for five years. They paid Innovative Market Systems $3 million for a 30 percent share in the new company.

Bloomberg's business was expanding and his family was, too. On January 1, 1983, a second daughter was born to Michael and Susan Bloomberg. They named her Georgina.

That same year, Bloomberg gave his mother an unusual birthday present to honor her on her seventy-fifth birthday. He donated the money to establish a professorship in her name at his alma mater, Johns Hopkins University. The professorship Bloomberg established at Johns Hopkins was called the Charlotte R. Bloomberg Professorship in the Humanities, which was in the university's Krieger School of Arts and Sciences.

With the sale of its terminals to Merrill Lynch, Innovative Market Systems had enough money to build additional terminals. And, in the financial community, interest was growing about getting up-to-the-minute data and information. By 1986 the company had outgrown its office space. Bloomberg rented a larger space and changed the company's name to Bloomberg L. P. By this time, he had placed more than 5,000 terminals on desks around New York City.

That same year he spent $3.5 million to buy a five-story town house on East Seventy-ninth Street in Manhattan. Bloomberg entertained lavishly in his new home. His guests included people like Barbara Walters, Beverly Sills, and other well-known people from the worlds of entertainment and business.

In January 1987, Bloomberg L. P. opened an office in London, England, and in May he opened one in Tokyo, Japan. Before long, the company had customers in many countries of the world. The Bank of England, the World Bank, and the Bank for International Settlements became customers, and the Vatican in Rome began to use the Bloomberg terminals. In the United States, the Federal Reserve Bank also began using them.

Bloomberg's first customer, Merrill Lynch, had 1,500 terminals installed on its traders' desks in its offices around the world. Michael Bloomberg later boasted, "By 1987, Merrill was poised

Political Profiles: **Michael Bloomberg**

to become the world's top underwriter [distributor] of stocks and bonds. . . . We helped Merrill get there."

By the following year, people in the securities industry were talking about Bloomberg's terminals. One of the people who wanted to know more about the company and its product was a reporter named Matthew Winkler. He arranged to write an article about it for the *Wall Street Journal*. With Michael Miller, a technology writer, Winkler got in touch with Michael Bloomberg and requested an interview.

New York City

Bloomberg knew that the publicity such an article would give his company would result in more business. "We've got the best people in the world working here," he told Winkler and Miller at the beginning of the interview. "All of them are workaholics. Once they come, they stay for the rest of their lives because they love it. They've built the better mousetrap. They're doing something important. Giving the little guy the information he needs to fight. Having fun. Staying ahead."

But the reporters wanted more information, so Bloomberg gave them the list of all his company's customers. "Here's every customer we have, by name, by firm, by phone number. Call them yourself!" Winkler called one of them, Robert Smith, who in 1988 managed the state of Florida's retirement system's money. "I'm working on a story about information technology on Wall Street and why money managers are using the Bloomberg system. I understand you have a Bloomberg terminal. What's so special about it?" Smith told him how easy the terminal was to use and how useful its information was to him.

The article ran in the *Wall Street Journal* on September 22, 1988. It told why Bloomberg's company was starting to challenge the giant Dow Jones & Company for dominance of the financial news market.

The article gave Bloomberg L. P. the publicity it wanted. But it brought with it a new problem that Bloomberg knew he needed to solve. How could he compete with a company like Dow Jones when his terminals only provided information about bonds?

Bloomberg called Matthew Winkler, the *Wall Street Journal* reporter, to get some advice. "I want to make our terminal indispensable to stock as well as bond traders. Should we get into the text news business?" Bloomberg asked. Text news would mean having news articles, not just the charts and graphs that the Bloomberg terminals provided.

Winkler replied, "Add text to that information and you'll have something that doesn't exist anywhere else. No one in debt or equity will be able to live without it." When the conversation was over, Bloomberg offered Winkler the job of running the new company. Winkler quickly accepted.

The Bloomberg Tower in New York City

Chapter 5

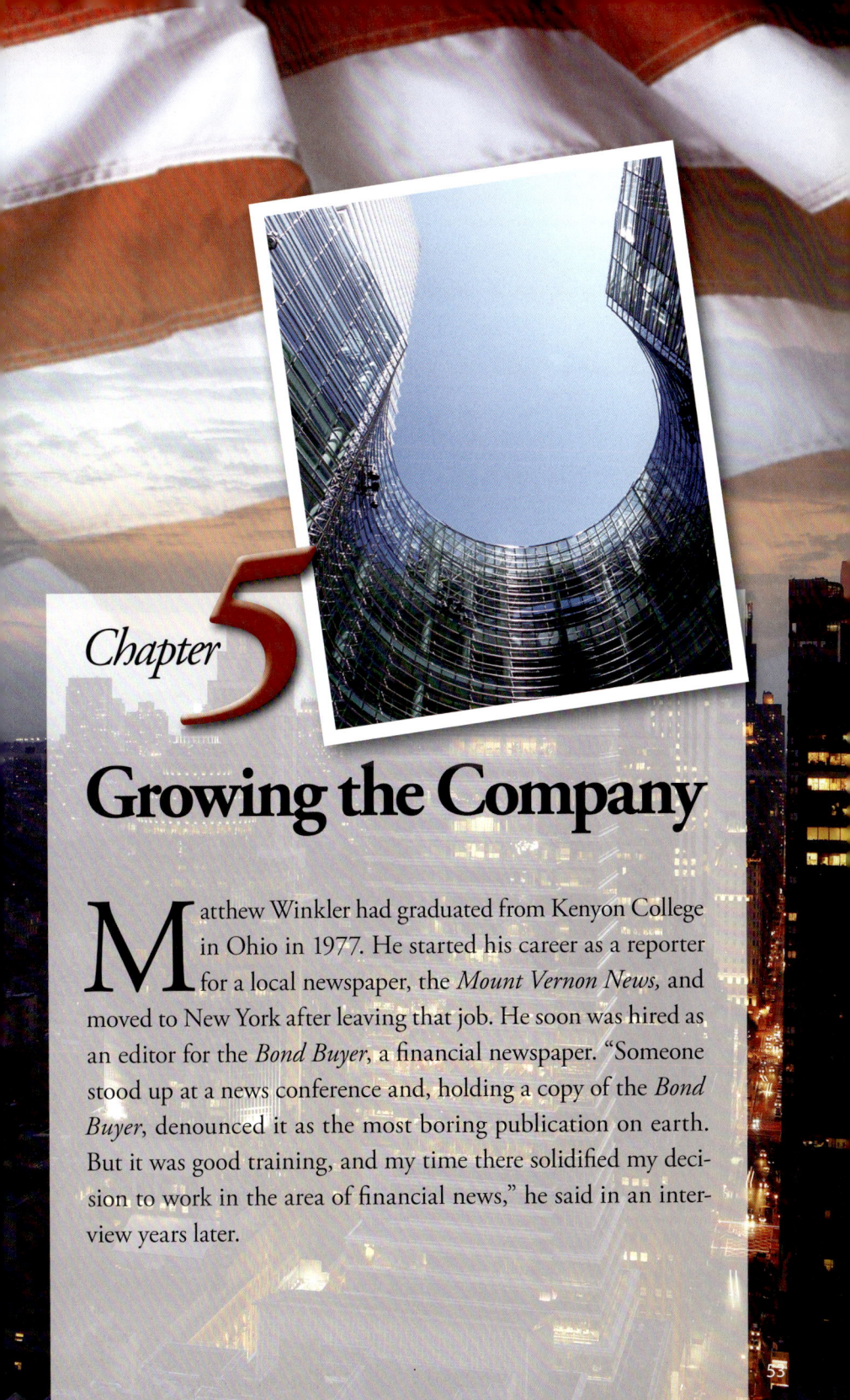

Growing the Company

Matthew Winkler had graduated from Kenyon College in Ohio in 1977. He started his career as a reporter for a local newspaper, the *Mount Vernon News,* and moved to New York after leaving that job. He soon was hired as an editor for the *Bond Buyer,* a financial newspaper. "Someone stood up at a news conference and, holding a copy of the *Bond Buyer,* denounced it as the most boring publication on earth. But it was good training, and my time there solidified my decision to work in the area of financial news," he said in an interview years later.

Political Profiles: **Michael Bloomberg**

In 1979 Winkler was hired as a reporter by Dow Jones & Company, which owned the *Wall Street Journal*. Based in both London and New York, Winkler wrote articles about the international financial markets. He came to work for Michael Bloomberg in 1990.

> *When I showed up at 8 A.M. to the Bloomberg office on the first day, Mike greeted me and said, 'Nice of you to show up!' I belatedly realized almost everyone had been at their desks for two hours at this fast moving company.... Also, I was impressed at the fact that they provided free soft drinks, water, coffees, teas, and snacks to everyone—those who work here and those who visit. And the company continues to do this today in all of its offices around the world.*

Bloomberg now had a news business company and Matthew Winkler to head it. He named the new company Bloomberg News Service.

Michael Bloomberg continued to sell his terminals, which now included news stories relating to business. Newspapers began to sign up to receive Bloomberg News stories, too. By March 1991, Bloomberg News employed more

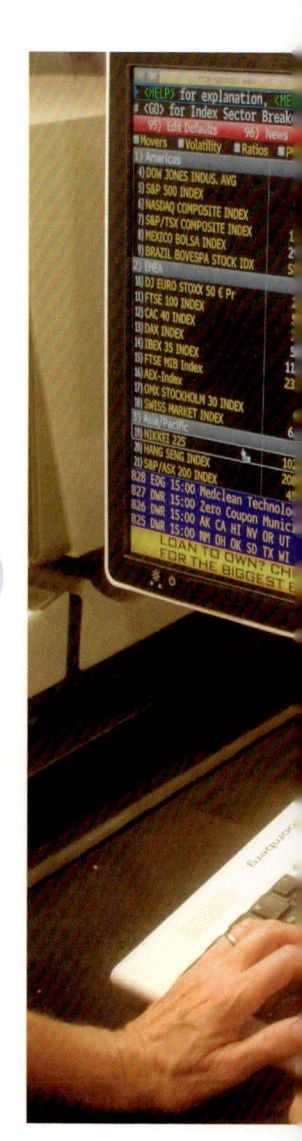

Growing the Company

than fifty reporters and had offices, called news bureaus, in New York, Princeton, New Jersey, Washington, D.C., London, Tokyo,

A Bloomberg data terminal. The Bloomberg Professional service allows financial industry workers the ability to monitor and analyze real-time financial market data, providing news and price quotes in addition to other services. This particular terminal is a display at the American Museum of Finance.

Bloomberg News service, London headquarters

and Toronto, Canada. A year later, Bloomberg News articles appeared in most major newspapers in the United States.

In 1992, Bloomberg built a TV studio in his Manhattan newsroom so that his reporters could tape interviews with people making news in the world of business. Bloomberg L. P. continued to grow and to expand, opening offices in Frankfurt, Germany, and Hong Kong.

The next step for Michael Bloomberg was to expand into radio and TV. The Financial News Network (FNN), a TV channel, was for sale. Jon Fram, who worked for FNN, called Bloomberg and suggested that he buy the network. "What a dumb idea," Bloomberg said, at first. He wasn't ready to buy a TV network. But, in 1992, he bought a New York City radio station, WNEW, which was for sale. He changed it to a news station, WBBR (for Bloomberg Business Radio). Then he ventured into TV, producing a daily thirty-minute A.M. show called *Bloomberg Business News* for Maryland Public TV. It was followed by weekly TV shows featuring business and finance stories and, finally, by Bloomberg Information Television, an all-news program.

Magazines and books followed. His first magazine was a monthly magazine called *Bloomberg Magazine*, which he started for the customers using his terminals, and Bloomberg Press began publishing books focused on business and finance.

Each time Bloomberg L. P. added another product or service, more people around the world became aware of the company and its products. By late 1993, there were 31,000 Bloomberg terminals sitting on desks around the world. Michael Bloomberg's business was doing very well. In 1997, he wrote his autobiography, *Bloomberg by Bloomberg*, with Matt Winkler's help.

Not everything that Michael Bloomberg tried to do turned out to be successful. In his personal life, things had changed. In

1993, after eighteen years of marriage, Michael Bloomberg and Susan Brown Bloomberg divorced. Their daughter Emma was twenty-one years old by then; Georgina was eighteen.

"We developed different interests, and as our daughters became more independent, the differences became more apparent," Bloomberg said. "I like skiing; she doesn't. She likes the movies; I don't. She likes to stay at home at night; I like to go out and party. . . . Business is a very important part of my life; she almost never came to visit my office. Nothing went wrong per se. . . . One day, we looked back and found things had changed. It was a slow evolution, but it happened."

Bloomberg and Susan remained good friends, despite the split. "Sue's a wonderful person, perhaps my closest friend and confidant," Bloomberg wrote in his 1997 biography. "And to this day we still do things with the kids as a unit, like weekend horse shows and holiday dinners together." One of their daughters said "my parents' divorce was one of the best things that ever happened to me. It made my relationship with both of my parents stronger. My parents are best friends."

Not everything in Bloomberg's business life was rock solid either. He tried to publish a monthly financial insert called *Bloomberg Personal*, to be distributed with Sunday newspapers, but that didn't work. So, in 1994, he and the editor changed the format to a second subscription-based magazine, which was successful.

In the mid-1990s, three female ex-employees filed sexual harassment lawsuits in Federal Court against Bloomberg and his company. One woman, who was pregnant, claimed Bloomberg told her to "Kill it!" Bloomberg denied under oath that he said such a thing; nevertheless, he settled the suit and admitted to making crude sexual comments to women employees. "We made a settlement and agreed not to talk about it," Bloomberg told a reporter.

By 2001, Bloomberg L. P. employed more than 7,000 people and had its business operations in 126 countries. Michael Bloomberg had become one of the wealthiest men in New York City.

But he was not content to just sit back and watch his empire grow. With a personal fortune at his disposal, Bloomberg turned to charitable giving—in the millions. He gave to the Jewish Museum in New York City, Johns Hopkins University, and Harvard. The money given to Harvard was used to establish a professorship in honor of Bloomberg's father, who had died in 1963, and for research, teaching, and course development in the areas of philanthropy, public service, and volunteering. These were things Michael Bloomberg's father had taught him were important when Michael was a boy. When he made the donation, Bloomberg praised his father as a person who "recognized the importance of reaching out to the nonprofit sector to help better the welfare of the entire community."

Through the Bloomberg Family Foundation, Bloomberg created the Initiative to Reduce Tobacco Use, also known as the Bloomberg Initiative. The Bloomberg Initiative supports government controls on tobacco use in countries such as China, India, and Bangladesh.

Michael Bloomberg had become not only one of the wealthiest people in the world but one of the most generous. In 2004 he donated $138 million to various charities, in 2005 $144 million, in 2006 $165 million, and in 2007, $205 million, making him the seventh-largest individual donor that year.

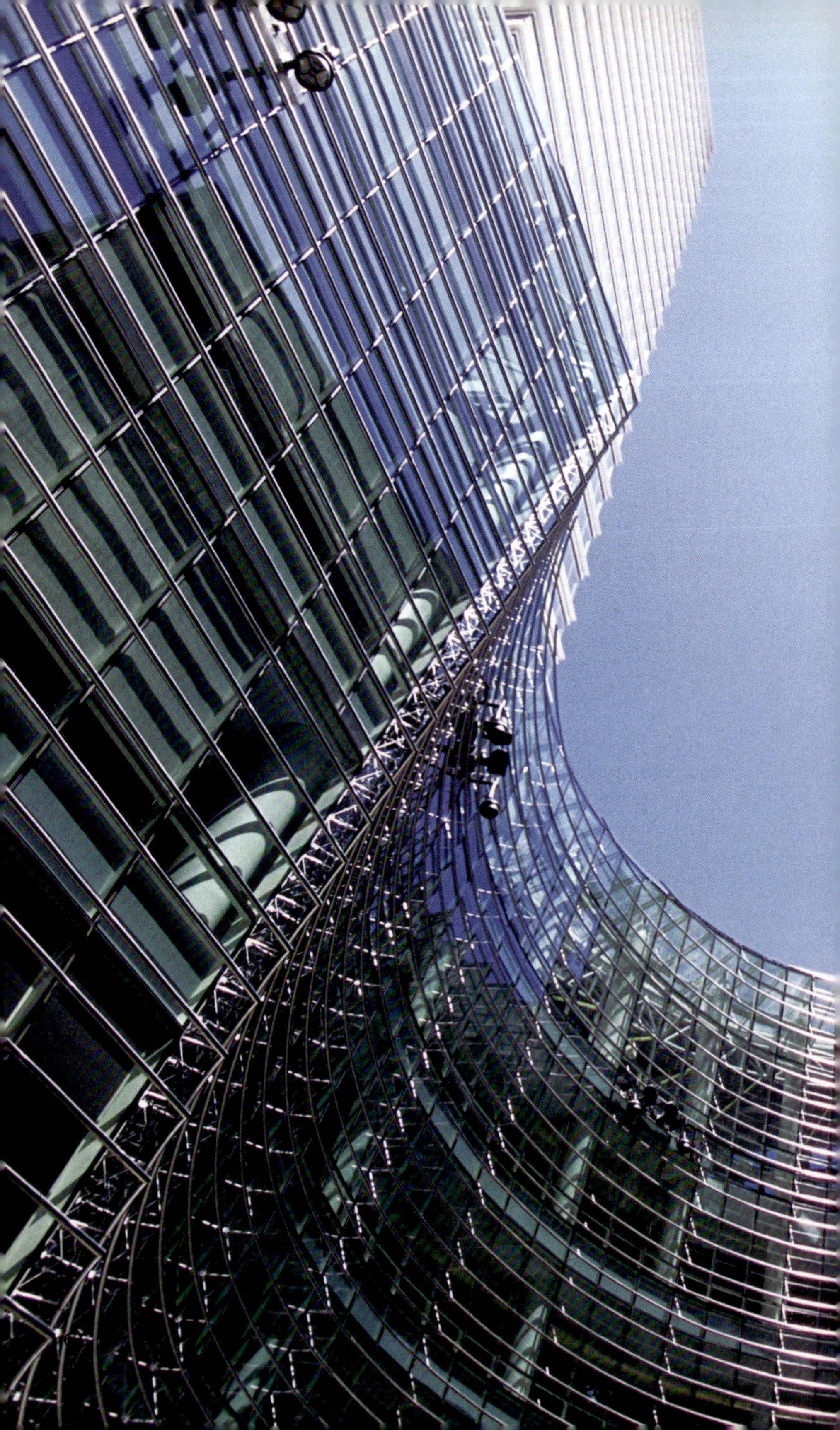

The Bloomberg building in New York

Political Profiles: **Michael Bloomberg**

Bloomberg also served on various boards, including those at the Lincoln Center for the Performing Arts and the Metropolitan Museum of Art in New York City.

In another area of Bloomberg's life, things were about to change. Seven years after the divorce from his wife, Bloomberg met Diana L. Taylor. They sat next to each other at a luncheon where he was the keynote speaker.

Born and raised in Old Greenwich, Connecticut, Taylor attended Milton Academy in Massachusetts, Dartmouth College, and Columbia University's School of Business. She began her career as an investment banker at Smith Barney, on Wall Street, and later would become New York State's superintendent of banks.

"I met the most fascinating man," Taylor told her mother. "Michael Bloomberg. We really had such a good time, and he is so smart and so nice. Probably he will never call me. . . ." But Bloomberg did call her, and they began dating. Later, Taylor moved into Bloomberg's Upper East Side town house, where they live today.

Opposite Page: Mayor Michael Bloomberg and his date Diana Taylor at Gracie Mansion for the wedding of former Mayor Rudolph Giuliani to Judith Nathan on Saturday, May 24, 2003, in New York. Bloomberg performed the ceremony.

63

New York City Council building

Chapter 6
Entering Public Service

In the late 1990s, Michael Bloomberg was looking for yet another new challenge. He had mentioned several times in interviews that, to him, the four best jobs in the world were president of the United States, secretary-general of the United Nations, president of the World Bank, and mayor of New York City. The first three jobs were already filled. But the mayoral election was coming up in New York City.

Rudolph Giuliani, New York City's mayor, was finishing his second term in office. He was prohibited by law to run for a third term. New York City voters voted in 1993 and then again in 1996 to impose term limits on mayors and members of the City Council, New York City's legislature. They could serve only two consecutive terms.

65

Michael Bloomberg with his daughter Emma after she graduated from Princeton University on June 5, 2001. Bloomberg announced his candidacy for mayor of New York City that same day.

Entering Public Service

Bloomberg spent millions of dollars of his own money to campaign for the office, promising, among other things, not to "take more that $1 a year from the city."

Once Bloomberg decided that he wanted to enter the mayoral race, he left Bloomberg L.P. in the hands of executives he trusted. New York City law prohibits an elected official, such as a mayor, to remain as the head of a company.

Historically, Democrats outnumber Republicans in New York by a huge margin. For that reason, New Yorkers don't usually elect Republican candidates. Bloomberg knew this. But there were four well-known Democratic candidates running in the Democratic primary. The winner would be the Democratic mayoral candidate in the general election. Bloomberg knew that he, an unknown candidate, would not have a chance to win if he entered the Democratic primary.

There was only one candidate running in the Republican primary. His name was Herman Badillo, and he was a former congressman and deputy mayor. So, Bloomberg decided to run as a Republican. "The polls tell me it's an uphill battle, but I can win," he told a reporter. "I don't have much experience with losing."

The primary election was scheduled for September 11, 2001. Because of the attack on the World Trade Center on that date, the primary elections were postponed for two weeks. Finally, registered Democrats and Republicans in New York City voted. The Democrats chose Mark Green

67

Political Profiles: **Michael Bloomberg**

to run as their candidate for mayor in the general election, and Republicans chose Michael Bloomberg. By the time the general election was held, Bloomberg had spent about $73 million of his own money in the campaign.

One of the first things Bloomberg had to learn was how to campaign for public office. He also had to convince the voters that he was just an ordinary man, even though he was a billionaire. He told a reporter, "You do get the question, 'What the [blank] do you have in common with me?' Well, the answer is that I've gotten fired from work, I've got fears about feeding the family and health and all of the things that everyone else has. I am over a lot of those because I have been very successful, but I was there." He added, "Am I lucky and successful and have a lot? Yes, absolutely. It doesn't mean I don't understand other people. I came to New York with debts and a dream."

During the campaign, Mark Green criticized Bloomberg for his lack of experience in government. "Him wanting to be mayor is like me going this afternoon to knock on the door of Bloomberg Inc. and saying, 'Hi, I'm Mark Green, I've never run a company for a day in my life, but I'd like to take over in four months. Where do I apply?'" Bloomberg countered, "It's no time for politics as usual," referring to the fact that Green and everyone else who ran in both the primary and the general elections had previously been in

New York Republican mayoral candidate Michael Bloomberg addressing supporters in New York's City Hall Park on August 22, 2001

Political Profiles: Michael Bloomberg

Mark Green

office and that they used money from the public to run their campaigns.

The general election was held on Tuesday, November 6, 2001. Bloomberg won by a margin of 50 percent to 48 percent. Some people thought he won because he outspent Green five-to-one. Others said it was because he had proved he knew how to run a business and that running the city was similar to running a business. Still others voted for him because he was a "fresh face" and not a politician, having never run for public office before.

Michael Bloomberg was sworn into office as New York City's 108th mayor on January 1, 2002. He refused to accept more than a $1 salary per year and did not move into Gracie Mansion, the traditional home of New York City's mayors. Instead, he remained in his five-story town house on East Seventy-ninth Street and traveled to City Hall when he needed to do the work of the city. He often traveled by subway, both to get to work fast and to show everyone that New York City's subways were safe and efficient.

Bloomberg became mayor just a few months after the September 11th attack on the World Trade Center. As a result, New York City was in a terrible financial crisis. It had already cost millions of dollars to start the cleanup of the World Trade Center site, to help victims of the attack and their families, and to provide other services that New Yorkers affected by the attack needed. Also, the city would receive fewer tax dollars from companies that had closed or moved out of the city after the attack and from the stock market, which was located near the attack site.

Despite the financial and psychological impact of the terrorist attacks on the city, Bloomberg was undeterred:

> *The real world, whether in business or government, requires that you don't jump to the endgame [or] to success right away. You do it piece by piece. Some people get immobilized when they come to a roadblock. My answer is, 'you know, it's a shame it's there, but now where else can we go? Let's just do it.'*

Smoke, flames, and debris erupt from one of the World Trade Center towers as a plane strikes it.

Bloomberg came into office faced with a budget gap of nearly $5 billion. As a result of the September 11th attack, the city lost 126,000 jobs in one year, and tax collections were expected to be down by $2 billion over two years. Bloomberg had few options: he could cut services, raise taxes, or both. He believed cutting back on services would send the wrong message to the business community and the outside world. So he raised property taxes (by 18.5 percent), a bold move that previous mayors hadn't dared to try in more than a decade.

In his first term, Bloomberg also passed an increase in cigarette taxes, to deter smoking; gained added control over education by winning the right to appoint members of the Board of Education; and hired a high-powered ad agency to promote New York, nationally and internationally, with a goal of luring 50 million visitors a year to the city by 2015. Foreign tourists spend three times as much as U.S. visitors to New York, so he also pushed for the opening of tourism offices around the world.

Bloomberg also set up a twenty-four hour customer-service line for New Yorkers to report everything from noise pollution to downed power lines. As a corporate executive, Bloomberg had always been responsive to his customers' needs, and he saw no reason why he shouldn't adopt the same attitude toward New Yorkers. Plus, the feedback would give him a sense of what was on the minds of his constituents, and whether problems were being solved.

To date, 311 has received more than 50 million calls, and two years after 311 was launched, inspections for excessive noise were up 94 percent and rodent extermination 36 percent.

Bloomberg also brought more openness to City Hall. In the same way that he set up a newsroom-style office at his company, Bloomberg decided to make City Hall and its agencies more

Mayor Bloomberg lays out his first city budget to members of the media on February 13, 2002, in New York's City Hall. Bloomberg's first budget, in the midst of the city's worst fiscal situation in years, would cut city departments by up to 26 percent to close a $4.76 billion deficit.

Entering Public Service

transparent as well. He arranged to have his desk and those of his staff clustered in a room without walls—and have glass doors installed throughout. Modeled on a trading floor, or bullpen, his desk is positioned in the middle.

"You've got to understand," he told a reporter. "My whole business life has been out in the open. If you put up barriers, physical barriers, people assume nefarious deeds are taking place on the other side. . . . If you don't have the barrier, [your employees think] yeah, you look like a decent guy."

New York City Hall

75

Fernando Ferrer (left), New York Democratic mayoral candidate, speaks as Republican incumbent Michael Bloomberg listens on November 1, 2005, in New York.

Chapter 7

Second Term Mayor

In 2005 Michael Bloomberg's term in office was coming to an end. He had to decide what he wanted to do. Should he run for a second term? Should he return to heading up Bloomberg L.P.? Should he do philanthropy full-time? Or should he do something entirely different, something he'd never done before?

Since he felt there was more that he could do for the city, he declared that he would run for a second term. This time he ran against a Democratic candidate, Fernando Ferrer, who was the borough president of the Bronx. New York City is divided into five parts, called boroughs—Manhattan, Brooklyn, Queens, the

Political Profiles: **Michael Bloomberg**

Bronx, and Staten Island. Each borough has a borough president, whose main job is to tell the mayor of New York City about the needs of their borough and the issues affecting it.

Every major newspaper in the city endorsed Bloomberg's reelection. Most labor unions also told its members to vote for him, as did many business groups and organizations. The election was held on November 8, 2005. By the time it was over, Bloomberg had beaten

A supporter holding a sign in front of New York Democratic mayoral candidate Fernando Ferrer, as Ferrer (right), campaigns in the Brooklyn borough of New York.

Mayor Bloomberg greeting supporters during a party for his election to a second term in New York on November 8, 2005

his competitor in every neighborhood in the city. Overall, Bloomberg defeated Ferrer by a 20 percent margin.

In his victory speech, Bloomberg said, "Tonight, we celebrate—tomorrow, we go back to work. We go back to fighting for a New York where families can live safely and grow, where the rights of every citizen are protected, a city where children can learn, with good jobs and housing and health care for all. I can't wait."

The following year, Bloomberg bought two adjacent town houses on Manhattan's Madison Avenue, which would become

Political Profiles: **Michael Bloomberg**

the headquarters of the Bloomberg Family Foundation. It would be the place from which he would continue his philanthropy.

In May 2007, Bloomberg went to Tufts University in his hometown of Medford, Massachusetts, to receive an honorary doctorate degree and to address the graduating class there. In his address, he listed his advice for the students:

"You gotta take risks."
"You can't do it alone."
"Give it to them straight."
"Respect others."
"The more you give, the more you get."

Then he added, "Don't forget to call your mother. I do every day." His mother, who was now ninety-eight years old, was seated in the audience. Bloomberg looked directly at her, and said, "Mother, I hope I'm not embarrassing you."

A month later, Bloomberg quit the Republican Party. With Republican president George W. Bush in the White House and Republicans in the majority in both the House of Representatives and the Senate, many Americans, including Michael Bloomberg, were unhappy with how the country was being governed.

Many people were against the war in Iraq and Republican policies directed toward the economy. Tax breaks were being given to big corporations in the hope that they would be used to hire more workers, build more factories, and make life easier for all Americans. Instead, the tax breaks were used to increase the salaries and bonuses given to executives who headed up those corporations, and jobs continued to be sent out of the country. Even though his personal wealth was not at stake, Bloomberg was not happy with what he saw happening in Washington, D.C.

He became an independent. That meant he wasn't affiliated with any political party. Candidates who run as independents normally don't win elections because they can't raise much money for their campaigns. So most voters don't know about the issues independent candidates believe in. Many don't even know that they're running for office. As a result, voters don't donate much money to help independent candidates get their message across. On the other hand, as an independent, Michael Bloomberg didn't need to raise money from the public. He had more than enough money of his own to pay for a campaign.

Almost immediately rumors started making the rounds that Bloomberg was considering a run for the White House when his term was over in 2009. (He wasn't allowed by law to run for a third term as mayor.) People were convinced that he would announce his intention to run for president when he gave speeches in which he made statements such as, "The people at both ends of Pennsylvania Avenue [referring to the White House and Congress] and on both sides of the aisle [referring to the Democrats and Republicans] just aren't facing up to the problems that need facing. The current situation is intolerable in Iraq. The public doesn't understand why we are there, and part of leadership is explaining, bringing people along." And, "You've got to stop nuclear proliferation, but I don't see any rational case for invasion or bombing [of Iran]."

But, then, on another occasion, the mayor told reporters, "I am not running for president. I have 790-odd days to go in this job, the greatest job in the world—maybe the second greatest job. The mayor's job is where you can really get things done.... I have been successful in business, and I hope when I leave this job they will say I was a good mayor or a great mayor."

Michael Bloomberg with his daughters Georgina (left) and Emma (right), at Emma's wedding in 2005. Emma, the eldest daughter, and Georgina have both worked on their father's campaigns. Emma deferred graduate school to work on Bloomberg's first campaign, and she has continued to be one of his hardest-working supporters.

83

Even so, the rumors that Bloomberg would run for president continued. Bloomberg himself did not put them to rest when he said, "I think that the candidates are not addressing, in a way at least I can understand, what they would do if they got elected. Unfortunately in the process that we go through—all of these, quote, 'debates'—you've got 30 seconds to tell us what you're going to do about the Iraq War, 30 seconds to tell us how to solve health care, 30 seconds on how to repair our relations around the world, 30 seconds on solving Social Security—there's no way to do that."

There was one major problem Bloomberg would face, should he announce a run for the White House. While most New Yorkers were happy with Bloomberg's anti-gun stance, there were some states in the U.S. where people were against gun control. It was feared that Bloomberg's involvement in the national Mayors Against Illegal Guns campaign would not sit well in those states. It might cause him to lose an election for president.

His mother, on the other hand, saw a different problem if her son ran for president. "I don't think this country is ready for a Jewish president," she said. "In the big cities there would be no problem because you have Jewish populations. But you get out in the middle of [the] country, where they have very few Jewish people, I'm afraid that is where you would see a lot of anti-Semitism."

But in February 2008 Bloomberg put the matter of his possible run for the presidency to rest. "I am not—and will not be—a candidate for president," he said.

Instead, the mayor continued his work to improve life in New York City. He tried to get a law passed that would make it more expensive for cars and trucks to go into midtown Manhattan, a very congested area of the city. The plan was called Congestion Pricing, and meant that vehicles entering a certain part of midtown Manhattan during the busiest hours of the day would have to pay for the privilege. Taxi, bus, and trucking companies, and even drivers of private automobiles, were against the plan and it was defeated.

For many years, Michael Bloomberg had been trying to convince people not to smoke. In July 2008, he teamed with Bill Gates, who had founded the Microsoft Corporation, to donate $500 million dollars to encourage people around the world to stop smoking or not to start smoking in the first place. "I'm an optimist, but I'm also a realist," he said at a news conference with Gates. "All the money in the world will never eradicate tobacco. But this partnership underscores how much the tide is turning against this deadly epidemic."

He explained what he and Gates wanted their partnership to accomplish. "This means assuring well-staffed tobacco control programs, raising tobacco taxes, running hard-hitting public information campaigns, creating comprehensive smoke-free public places, and banning tobacco advertising," he said.

During his second term in office, Bloomberg balanced the city's budget. He continued to reform education, something he'd started during his first term. Unemployment fell to a record low. He mandated, or ordered, the Welfare to Work Initiative, whereby as many people receiving welfare payments who could be trained for a job received training—and many got jobs. The city supplemented their wages so they would have enough money to live on. Even so, the cost of providing welfare for poor families in the city was reduced. As a member of a group of mayors from all over the country, Bloomberg worked to try to keep illegal guns off city streets and out of the hands of criminals.

In his second term, he continued to build on the successes of his first four years. He worked to keep New York City's economy strong in spite of the downturn in the world economy. He announced plans to rebuild old, neglected areas of the city, so businesses could open and people could live there. He worked to keep the city's streets safe, and he continued to improve public education for the children of New York City.

But rumors about Bloomberg's future plans continued to swirl. On November 6, 2007, the rumor was that he would run for election as governor of New York State in the 2010 election. Bloomberg denied that he had any such intention.

His life continued to be a hectic round of official mayoral duties by day and social events during the evening. With Diana Taylor at his side, he hosted dinner parties and attended dinners and parties given by others. "That's what you do in New York when you reach a certain level of economic success," an old friend of Bloomberg's said. "If you want to be on the circuit, which is defined as going to all those stupid dinners every night in black tie, if you wanted to be seen, you show up." From all the social engagements Bloomberg attended, it was obvious that he enjoyed being out and about socially. From time to time, he even escaped for a weekend of golf in Bermuda, where he has a home.

All of this excitement finally took a toll on the mayor, who was now more than sixty years old. Halfway through his second term in office, he had stents put into a blocked artery leading away from his heart. A stent is a wire tube that opens up the blocked artery, allowing blood to flow easily through it. It was not until a couple of years later that Bloomberg, who was always silent about his private life, let the public know that he'd had the stents put in.

Second Term Mayor

On October 2, 2008, Michael Bloomberg made an announcement that no one had anticipated. He had decided what he wanted to do when his second term as mayor of New York City ended, and that was to run for a third term.

Diana Taylor and Mayor Bloomberg at the Ralph Lauren Fortieth Anniversary Commemorative Fashion Show and Black Tie Dinner held in Central Park Conservatory Gardens on September 8, 2007, in New York

The Empire State Building

Chapter 8

Defying Tradition

Michael Bloomberg had a year left of his second term as the 108th Mayor of New York City. On October 2, 2008, he announced that he was going to ask the City Council, New York City's legislature, to amend, or change, the law that allowed the mayor and members of the City Council to serve only two terms in office. He wanted to run for a third term.

"Given the events of recent weeks and given the enormous challenges we face, I don't want to walk away from a city I feel I can help lead through these tough times," he explained, referring to the slowdown in the economy. He felt that there was still so much that he could do to guide New York City out of this recession. "Handling this financial crisis while strengthening essential services . . . is a challenge I want to take on," he said.

Many people both inside and outside of government were shocked—and angry. Bloomberg was accused of being undemocratic and of not respecting the wishes of the people of New York. After all, they had twice voted to restrict their elected officials to two terms in office. But Bloomberg insisted, "You're not taking away term limits. You're simply going from two terms to three terms." Many members of the City Council agreed with him. After all, that meant that they could serve a third term in office as well.

Some people thought that changing term limits should be put to the voters in a special election to be held in late winter or in early spring of 2009. The mayor considered a special vote unnecessary, since the mayoral election was already scheduled for November 2009. He explained, "I want to give the voters a chance to decide if they want me at the helm. If voters don't like what they've seen, they will vote for someone else."

Among those who were thinking of running for mayor in 2009 was William Thompson, the city's comptroller, who was in charge of protecting the pension funds of New York City employees. He had heard Bloomberg say he approved of the term limits the voters had agreed on and did not like the fact that he had changed his mind. "I am disappointed," he said. "I have over a period of years taken the mayor at his word. I just think this is a whole attempt to undermine democracy."

On October 23, the members of the City Council voted 29-22 in favor of extending term limits from two to three terms. Public hearings were held, where ordinary people could speak out for or against extending term limits. Many said they thought that allowing the mayor to run for a third term would give him time to complete all the work he'd begun in 2001, when he was elected to his first term. Others thought that after a second term in office, it was time for a change and that it would be better to have a new person take over the job. But, on November 3, Bloomberg signed the bill to extend term limits into law.

As soon as he had signed the bill into law, Michael Bloomberg began campaigning for his third term as mayor. He wanted to reform the Metropolitan Transportation Authority, the organization responsible for running the buses and trains. He promised to put up-to-date bus and train information on the 311 Call Center, so commuters would know in advance if the bus or subway train they needed to ride in was late or was running on time.

Even though his congestion pricing plan, which called for charging motorists to drive into midtown Manhattan, had been defeated, Bloomberg continued to be concerned about the traffic congestion in that area. "The midtown traffic mess is one of those problems everyone always talks about," he said. "Well, we're not just going to sit back—we're going to try to do something about it." He was in favor of providing free crosstown bus service in midtown Manhattan as a way to make traffic move more quickly. He wanted to keep cars, trucks, and buses off Broadway, a major avenue, where it runs through midtown Manhattan.

He visited various sections of the city and spoke to groups of African Americans, Hispanics, older New Yorkers, and women. "I'm going to work as hard as I can for this city for the next 150-odd days [the number of days left in his second term] and campaign as hard as I can for the next 96- or 97-odd days [the number of days until the next election], and if the public wants me to keep working, they have a chance to express that on Nov. 3 [Election Day]," he told the voters.

Heavy traffic on Franklin D. Roosevelt East River Drive in New York

Defying Tradition

New York City Comptroller and Democratic mayoral candidate William Thompson, Jr., addresses the moderator, NY-1 News anchor Dominic Carter (left), as Thompson's opponent, New York City councilman Tony Avella, listens during the Democratic Mayoral Debate at the New York Public Library on August 26, 2009, in New York.

Like he had during his first two mayoral campaigns, Bloomberg accepted no money from people or organizations. Again, he funded his campaign with his own money. By the middle of August, he had spent $36 million.

On September 15, the Democrats held their primary election and selected William Thompson as their choice to run against Michael Bloomberg in the general election. The Republicans did not have to hold a primary election. That is because Bloomberg

Political Profiles: **Michael Bloomberg**

was running as a Republican as well as an Independent. And because he was the incumbent, or the person holding the office at the time, he did not have to run in a primary election.

Defying Tradition

At times, the campaign got ugly between Thompson and Bloomberg. Thompson's campaign, for example, adopted the slogan "Eight Is Enough," meaning that two terms (eight years

New York City Mayor Michael Bloomberg and his challenger, city comptroller William Thompson, Jr., speak during the first mayoral debate on October 13, 2009, in New York.

in office) should be all that Bloomberg gets. They also accused Bloomberg of contributing money to many organizations so they would endorse him and urge their members to vote for him.

Voters were angry at Bloomberg and the City Council for changing term limits. They showed their dissatisfaction in the primary election. They voted several City Council members who had voted to change term limits out of office. But many voters thought Bloomberg was a good mayor and said they would vote for him anyway.

By October 3, just one month before the general election, Michael Bloomberg had spent almost $65 million of his own money on his campaign. Thompson, whose money came mostly from contributions from voters who wanted him to win, had spent under $4 million.

Meanwhile, important people and organizations endorsed both Bloomberg and Thompson. Former mayor Rudolph Giuliani, a Republican, endorsed Michael Bloomberg and campaigned for him. In one campaign speech, Bloomberg told his audience, "We all benefited from his [Giuliani's] leadership, and our city is a much better place because of it." In a piece of campaign literature mailed out to voters, Giuliani is quoted as saying, "If you want the progress to continue, vote and re-elect Mike Bloomberg."

On the other hand, a spokesman for President Barack Obama, Governor David Paterson of New York, and both of New York's U. S. senators, all of whom are Democrats, endorsed Thompson.

On Election Day, only about 1.1 million people out of 4.5 million eligible New Yorkers went to the polls. Many New Yorkers said they believed that Bloomberg was sure to win, so why should they bother about going out to vote.

When all the votes were counted, Michael Bloomberg *did* win a third term, but not by the wide margin that had been predicted. He won by five percentage points. Only 51,000 more people voted for him than voted for William Thompson.

But, to Michael Bloomberg, it was a victory and that's what counted. He now had four more years in which to complete the work he'd started in 2001 for the people of New York. Moreover, there was still the possibility of an independent run for the Oval Office in 2012.

> *I'm not a political guy. I've never watched any [election campaign] television debates, I've never had a great interest in politics. The challenge of making life better for people, that's not politics so much as government.*

Mayor Bloomberg soon had a chance to prove he was still determined to not be a typical mayor. In the summer of 2010 a controversy erupted over the building of an Islamic mosque and community center two blocks from where the World Trade Center had stood. Polls showed that a majority of New Yorkers were opposed to the plan. But Michael Bloomberg argued that freedom of religion is a fundamental right for all Americans. When the city's Landmarks Commission approved the construction on August 3, 2010, the mayor said in a public announcement:

Whatever you may think of the proposed mosque and community center, lost in the heat of the debate has been a basic question: Should government attempt to deny private citizens the right to

Political Profiles: **Michael Bloomberg**

Should government attempt to deny private citizens the right to build a house of worship on private property based on their particular religion? That may happen in other countries, but we should never allow it to happen here. This nation was founded on the principle that the government must never choose between religions, or favor one over another.

Although it was not the expedient thing to do, Michael Bloomberg made it clear he thought some things are more important than politics. On this issue, he was not going to act like "a political guy."

Mayor Bloomberg (center), City Council Speaker Christine Quinn (fourth from left), and members of local religious institutions stand in front of the Statue of Liberty for a news conference in New York on August 3, 2010. The political and religious leaders were there to show their support for a mosque and Islamic cultural center planned in lower Manhattan.

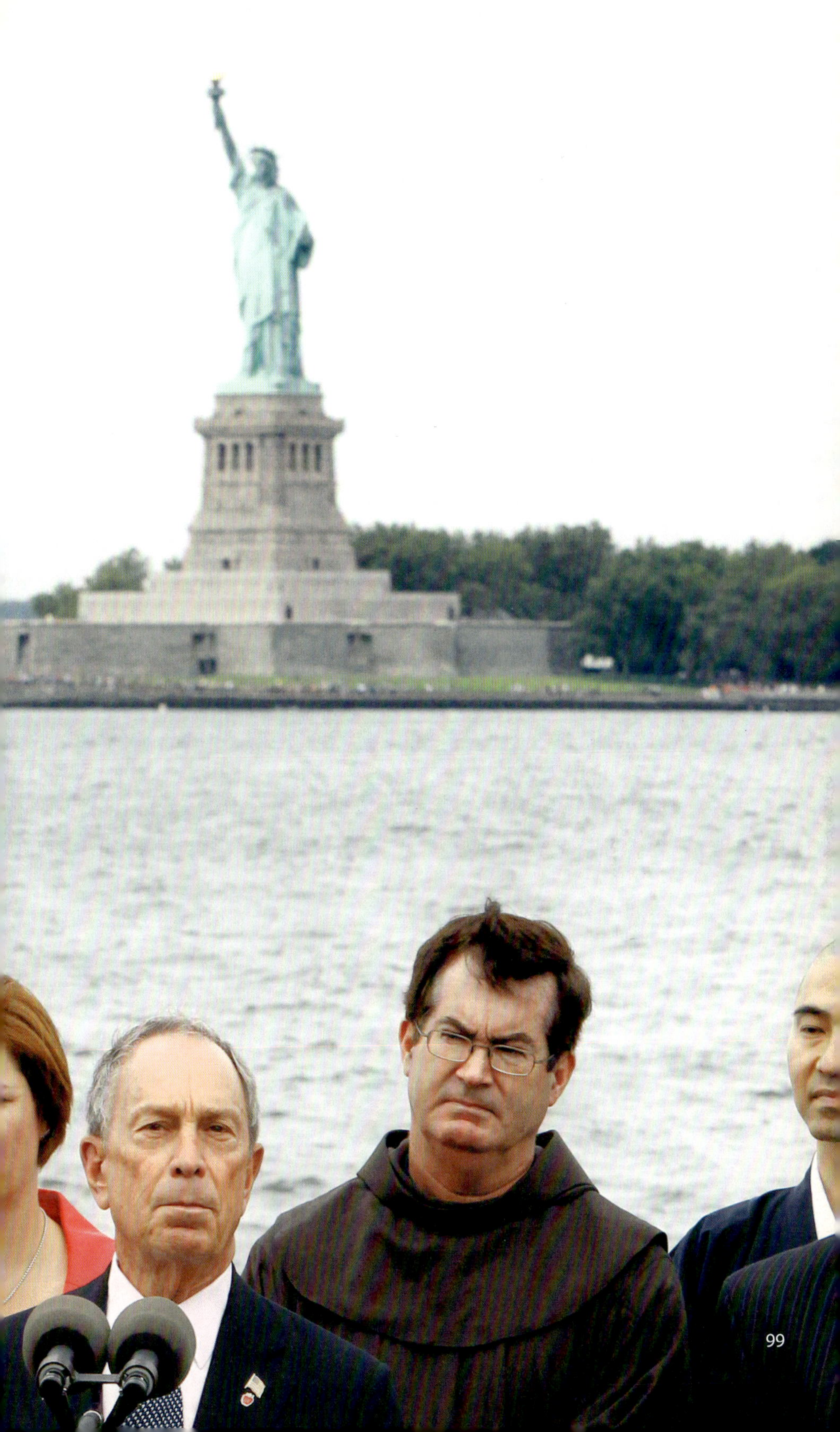

Timeline

1942
Born in Boston, Massachusetts, on February 14.

1944
Sister Marjorie is born.

1960
Graduates from high school in Medford, Massachusetts, on June 3.

1963
Father dies.

1964
Graduates from Johns Hopkins University with degree in electrical engineering.

1966
Graduates from Harvard University with masters in business administration; goes to work for Salomon Brothers & Hutzler, a financial firm, in New York City.

1970
Begins to build prototype desktop terminal for Salomon Brothers.

1972
Becomes a partner at Salomon Brothers.

1975
Marries Susan Brown.

1979
Daughter Emma is born.

1981
Loses job at Salomon Brothers when it merges with Philco Corporation; gets $10 million in severance pay.

1981
Starts own company, Innovative Market Systems; builds enhanced desktop terminals, later called Bloombergs.

1982
Sells first twenty terminals to Merrill Lynch & Company.

1983
Daughter Georgina is born; donates large sum of money to John's Hopkins University in honor of mother's seventy-fifth birthday.

1986
Innovative Market Systems becomes Bloomberg L. P.

1987
Bloomberg L. P. expands to countries overseas.

1990
Hires Matthew Winkler to head Bloomberg News Service.

1992
Bloomberg News Service adds TV and radio components.

1993
Divorces after eighteen years of marriage.

1996
Donates large sum of money to Harvard University in honor of father.

2000
Meets Diana L. Taylor.

2001
Runs for office of mayor of New York City; spends more than $70 million of own money during campaign.

2002
Inaugurated as New York City's 108th mayor on January 3.

2005
Successfully runs for second term as mayor.

2009
Wins third term as mayor after two-term limit law is changed.

Political Profiles: **Michael Bloomberg**

Sources

Chapter One: "Just a Regular Kid"

p. 11,   "I had stirred the pot . . ." Dean E. Murphy, "Man in the News; Finding a New Mission; Michael Rubens Bloomberg," *New York Times*, November 7, 2001.

p. 12,   "of liberal views . . ." Michael R. Blood, "From Mogul to Mayor Mike Makes His Mark," *New York Daily News*, Novemeer 7, 2001.

p. 13,   "our lawyer . . ." Joyce Purnick, "Mike Bloomberg," *New York Times*, October 9, 2009.

p. 13,   "to strive relentlessly . . ." Blood, "From Mogul to Mayor Mike Makes His Mark."

p. 13,   "Nobody on the street . . ." Ibid.

p. 13,   "a regular kid . . ." Ibid.

p. 13,   "I had discipline problems . . ." Joyce Purnick, *Mike Bloomberg: The Mogul and the Mayor* (New York: PublicAffairs, 2009), 20-21.

p. 13,   "anything that came along . . ." Purnick, "Mike Bloomberg."

p. 15,   "Perhaps the proudest . . ." Jon Meacham, "The Revolutionary," *Newsweek*, November 12, 2007.

p. 18,   "What the hell . . ." Murphy, "Man in the News; Finding a New Mission; Michael Rubens Bloomberg."

p. 19,   "Great. Got in . . ." Michael Bloomberg, *Bloomberg by Bloomberg* (New York: John Wiley & Sons, Inc., 1997, 2001), 13.

p. 19,   "What's the point? . . ." Ibid.

Sources

Chapter Two: Off to Graduate School

p. 21-22, "In graduate school . . ." Meacham, "The Revolutionary."
p. 23, "I've always felt . . ." Ibid.
p. 23, "Who are they? . . ." Bloomberg, *Bloomberg by Bloomberg*, 15.
p. 24, "Look, I can't afford . . ." Ibid., 18.

Chapter Three: Working on Wall Street

p. 28, "a meritocracy . . ." Dave Saltonstall, "Maverick Mogul Eyes City Hall," *New York Daily News*, March 18, 2001.
p. 32, "We could sell . . ." Elizabeth Kolbert, "The Mogul Mayor," *New Yorker*, April 22 & 29, 2002, 141.
p. 32, "I didn't love Wall Street . . ." Murphy, "Man in the News; Finding a New Mission; Michael Rubens Bloomberg."
p. 33, "I'm told . . ." Bloomberg, *Bloomberg by Bloomberg*, 132-133.
p. 34, "But you can only . . ." Ibid., 133.
p. 34, "I'll quit . . ." Ibid., 33.
p. 38, "That's what all . . ." Michael Daly, "Pilot Mike Steers Us From Peril," *New York Daily News*, June 15, 2005.
p. 38, "I think I remember . . ." Dean E. Murray, "Bloomberg a Man of Contradictions, but With a Single Focus," *New York Times*, November 26, 2001.
p. 40, "He got put . . ." Purnick, *Mike Bloomberg: The Mogul and the Mayor*, 33.
p. 41, "I got into the car . . ." Harvey Mackay, *We Got Fired! ...And It's the Best Thing That Ever Happened to Us* (New York: Ballantine Books, 2004), 212.

Political Profiles: **Michael Bloomberg**

Chapter Four: Going It Alone

p. 44, "It'll mean . . ." Bloomberg, *Bloomberg by Bloomberg*, 211.

p. 45, "four guys . . ." "Michael Bloomberg: Inspiration for Innovation," CME Group Magazine, Spring 2008, http://www.cmegroup.com/company/history/magazine/Spring2008/michaelbloomberg.html.

p. 45, "We all worked . . ." Tom Secunda, interview by Judith Czelusniak of Bloomberg L. P., August 19, 2009.

p. 45, "I've always thought . . ." Meacham, "The Revolutionary."

p. 46, "I remember . . ." Bloomberg, "Bloomberg: Inspiration for Innovation."

p. 46, "We're out of control . . ." Bloomberg, *Bloomberg by Bloomberg*, 54.

p. 47-48, "By 1987 . . ." Leah Nathans Spiro, "In Search of Michael Bloomberg," *BusinessWeek*, May 5, 1997.

p. 50, "We've got the best people . . ." Bloomberg, *Bloomberg by Bloomberg*, 72-73.

p. 50, "Here's every customer . . ." Ibid., 73.

p. 50, "I'm working . . ." Ibid.

p. 50, "I want to make . . ." Ibid., 76.

p. 51, "Add text . . ." Ibid.

Chapter Five: Growing the Company

p. 53, "Someone stood up . . ." Linda Michaels, "Winkler's luck: A decision to cast his fate with Michael Bloomberg pays off for Matthew Winkler," *Kenyon College Alumni Bulletin* 20, no. 4 (November 4, 1998), http://bulletin.kenyon.edu/x1571.xml.

p. 54, "When I showed up . . ." Matthew Winkler, interview by Judith Czelusniak of Bloomberg L. P., August 17, 2009.

Sources

p. 57, "What a dumb . . ." Bloomberg, *Bloomberg by Bloomberg*, 114.

p. 58, "We developed . . ." Ibid., 213.

p. 58, "Sue's a wonderful . . ." Saltonstall, "Maverick Mogul Eyes City Hall."

p. 58, "my parents' divorce . . ." Murphy, "Bloomberg a Man of Contradictions, but With a Single Focus."

p. 58-59, "Kill it! . . ." Mark Gimein, Doris Burke, Elias Rodriguez, and Noshua Watson, "Mayor Mogul," *Fortune*, April 1, 2002.

p. 59, "recognized the importance . . ." "Michael R. Bloomberg," National Eagle Scout Association, 2008, http://www.nesa.org/bloomberg.html.

p. 62, "I met the most . . ." Heidi Evans, "She's Not Just His 'Gal Pal,'" *New York Daily News*, August 13, 2007.

Chapter Six: Entering Public Service

p. 67, "The polls . . ." Matt Bai, "Out of the Box," *Newsweek*, April 30, 2001.

p. 68, "You do get . . ." Dave Saltonstall, "Mike's making the city his business," *New York Daily News*, August 29, 2001.

p. 68, "Am I lucky . . ." Ibid.

p. 68, "Him wanting to be . . ." Bai, "Out of the Box."

p. 68, "It's no time . . ." Blood, "From Mogul to Mayor Mike Makes His Mark."

p. 71, "The real world . . ." Tom Lowry, "The CEO Mayor," *BusinessWeek*, June 25, 2007.

p. 75, "You've got to . . ." Gimein, Burke, Rodriguez, and Watson, "Mayor Mogul."

Chapter Seven: Second Term Mayor

p. 79, "Tonight, we celebrate . . ." Patrick D. Healy, "Bloomberg Cruises to Re-election Victory," *New York Times*, November 9, 2005.

p. 80, "You gotta . . ." James Vaznis, "Among NYC mayor's advice to grads: Call your mother," *Boston Globe*, May 21, 2007.

p. 80, "Mother, I hope . . ." Ibid.

p. 81, "The people . . ." Meacham, "The Revolutionary," 2007.

p. 81, "I am not running . . ." Ibid.

p. 84, "I think that the candidates . . ." Ibid.

p. 84, "I don't think . . ." Purnick, *Mayor Mike: The Mogul and the Mayor*, 14.

p. 84, "I am not . . ." Andrew Stevens, "Michael Bloomberg: Mayor of New York," *City Mayors: U.S. Mayors*, October 25, 2008, http://www.citymayors.com/mayors/new_york_mayor.html.

p. 85, "I'm an optimist . . ." Donald G. McNeil, Jr., "Pledging $500 Million, Bloomberg And Gates Take Aim at Smoking," *New York Times*, July 24, 2008.

p. 86, "That's what you do . . ." Purnick, *Mayor Mike: The Mogul and the Mayor*, 61.

Chapter Eight: Defying Tradition

p. 89-90, "Given the events . . ." Adam Lisberg, "Mayor Bloomberg makes it official: I'm going to seek third term," *New York Daily News*, October 3, 2008.

p. 90, "You're not . . ." Alex Altman, "Term Limits," *Time*, October 3, 2008.

p. 90, "I want to give . . ." Lisberg, "Mayor Bloomberg makes it official: I'm going to seek third term."

Sources

p. 90, "I am disappointed . . ." Ibid.

p. 91, "The midtown traffic mess . . ." Nick Summers, "Where the Neon Lights Are Bright—And Drivers Are No Longer Welcome," *Newsweek*, March 9, 2009.

p. 91, "I'm going to work . . ." Celeste Katz, "Mike might even mull a fourth term," *New York Daily News*, August 2, 2009.

p. 96, "We all benefited . . ." "Rudy Giuliani Stumps For Bloomberg In NYC," October 8, 2009, http://wcbstv.com/local/giuliani.bloomberg.mayor.2.1255634.html.

p. 97, "I'm not a political guy . . ." Gimein, Burke, Rodriguez, and Watson, "Mayor Mogul."

Political Profiles: **Michael Bloomberg**

Bibliography

Bloomberg, Michael. *Bloomberg by Bloomberg.* New York: John Wiley & Sons, Inc., 1997, 2001.

Fink, Anne-Marie. *The Money Makers: How Extraordinary Managers Win in a World Turned Upside Down.* New York: Crown Business, 2009.

Gant, Scott. *We're All Journalists Now: The Transformation of the Press and Reshaping of the Law in the Internet Age.* New York: Free Press, 2007.

Geisst, Charles R. *The Last Partnerships: Inside the Great Wall Street Money Dynasties.* New York: McGraw-Hill, 2001.

Geisst, Charles R. *100 Years of Wall Street.* New York: McGraw-Hill, 2000.

Harper, Steven C. *The McGraw-Hill Guide to Starting Your Own Business.* New York: McGraw-Hill, Inc., 1991.

Kivelson, Adrienne. *What Makes New York City Run: A Citizen's Guide to How City Government Works.* New York: The League of Women Voters of the City of New York Education Fund, 1979, 1991, 2001.

Lewis, Michael. *Liar's Poker: Rising Through the Wreckage on Wall Street.* New York: W. W. Norton & Company, 1989.

Poteet, Dr. G. Howard, compiler. *Starting Up Your Own Business: Expert Advice from the Small Business Administration.* New York: Liberty Hall Press, 1991.

Purnick, Joyce. *Mike Bloomberg: Money, Power, Politics.* New York: PublicAffairs, 2009.

Ritchie, Donald A. *Reporting From Washington: The History of the Washington Press Corps.* New York: Oxford University Press, 2005.

Sobel, Robert. *Salomon Brothers 1910-1985: Advancing to Leadership.* New York: Salomon Brothers Inc. 1986.

———. *The Big Board: A History of the New York Stock Market.* The Free Press, 1965 (Reprinted by Beard Books, Washington, D.C., 2000).

Stern, Ellen. *Gracie Mansion; A Celebration of New York City's Mayoral Residence.* New York: Rizzoli International Publications, Inc., 2005.

Web sites

http://www.mikebloomberg.com
The official Web site of Michael Bloomberg. Includes his record as mayor, his vision for the future of the city, his biography, videos, and news articles.

http://www.nyc.gov
The official Web site of New York City contains information about elected city officials and city services.

http://www.bloomberg.com
This is an online service that provides business news and information.

Book cover and interior design by Derrick Carroll Creative.

Political Profiles: **Michael Bloomberg**

Index

311 Call Center, 73, 91

Badillo, Herman, 67
Bloomberg, Charlotte (mother), 12–13, *14,* 15, *16,* 30, 47, 80
Bloomberg, Emma (daughter), 40, 58, *66–67, 82–83*
Bloomberg, Georgina (daughter), 46, 58, *82–83*
Bloomberg, Marjorie (sister), 12, *14, 16*
Bloomberg, Michael, *2, 8, 10, 14, 16–17, 20, 36–37, 63, 66–67, 68–69, 74, 76, 79, 82–83, 87, 94–95, 98–99*
   Bloomberg by Bloomberg (autobiography), 57
   campaign finances, 68, 70, 93, 96
   character, 13, 59
   childhood, 12–15
   and computers, 33–34, 40
   education, 13, 15, 18–19, 21–22
   entrepreneurship, 44–47
   fatherhood, 40, 46, 58
   financial career, 23–24, 27–30, 32–34, 33, 38, 40–41
   health, 86
   international offices, 47, 55, 57
   marriage, 38, 58
   as Mayor, 71, 73, 75, 84–86, 97–98
   mayoral race, first, 67–68, 70
   mayoral race, second, 77–79
   mayoral race, third, 87, 89–91, 93–97

   philanthropy, 15, 18, 30, 59, 77, 80
   political affiliations, 67, 80–81, 94, 97
   and sexual harassment, 58
   social life, 47, 62, 86
   wealth, 59, 68, 81, 93
Bloomberg, Susan Brown (former wife), 38, 40, 44, 46, 58
Bloomberg, William (father), 12–13, *14, 16,* 30, 59
Bloomberg Business News, 57
Bloomberg Business Radio, 57
Bloomberg Family Foundation, 59, 80
Bloomberg Information Televison, 57
Bloomberg Initiative, 59
Bloomberg L. P., 47, 50, 57, 59, 67, 77
Bloomberg Magazine, 57
Bloomberg News, 54–55, 57
Bloomberg News Service, 54, *56*
Bloomberg Personal, 58
Bloomberg Press, 57
Bloomberg terminals, 44–48, 50, 54, *54–55,* 57
Bloomberg Tower, *52, 60–61*

Congestion Pricing Plan, 84–85, 91

Dow Jones & Co., 50, 54

Ferrer, Fernando, *76,* 77, *78,* 79
Financial News Network (FNN), 57

Gates, Bill, 84–85
Giuliani, Rudolf, 65, 96
Goldman, Sachs & Company, 23
Green, Mark, 67–68, 70, *70*
Ground Zero, 97–98
gun control, 84, 86

Index

Gutfreund, John, 23–24, 32–34
Harvard Business School, *18–19*, 19, 21, *25*, 59
Initiative to Reduce Tobacco Use, 59
Innovative Market Systems, 44–47
Iraq War, 80–81, 84
Islamic cultural center, 97–98, *98–99*

Johns Hopkins University, 15, 47, 59

Landmarks Commission, 97–98

MacMillan, Duncan, 44
mayors, term limits for, 65, 89–91, 96
Mayors Against Illegal Guns, 84
Merrill Lynch, 45–48
Metropolitan Transportation Authority, 91
Miller, Michael, 48, 50
New York Stock Exchange, 28, 30, *31*

Paterson, David, 96
Perry, Jay, 38, 40

Rosenthal, Richard, 38, 40
Salomon, William, 24, 28, 32–34
Salomon Brothers & Hutzler, 11, 23, 27–28, 30
Salomon's Information Systems, 40
Secunda, Tom, 44–45
Smith, Robert, 50
smoking and tobacco, 59, 73, 85

Taylor, Diana L. (girlfriend), 59, *63*, 86, *87*

Thompson, William, 90, 93, *93, 94–95*, 95–97
Tufts University, 80

Vietnam War, *22*, 22–23

WBBR radio station, 57
Welfare to Work Initiative, 85
Winkler, Matthew, 48, 50–51, 53–54, 57
World Trade Center, 67, 71, *72*, 73

Zegar, Chuck, 44

111

Political Profiles: **Michael Bloomberg**

Credits

2: Evan Agostini/PictureGroup via AP IMAGES
8-9: Office of the Mayor, City of New York
10: Office of the Mayor, City of New York
14: Office of the Mayor, City of New York
16-17: Office of the Mayor, City of New York
18-19: Philip Scalia / Alamy
20: Office of the Mayor, City of New York
22: Courtesy of the U.S. Army
23: Courtesy of the Library of Congress
25: Courtesy of Chensiyuan
26-27: Used under license from iStockphoto.com
28-29: Used under license from iStockphoto.com
31: Courtesy of the National Park Service
34-35: Used under license from iStockphoto.com
36-37: AP Photo
39: Used under license from iStockphoto.com
40-41: Courtesy of Daniel Schwen
42: Used under license from iStockphoto.com
45: Courtesy of Boffy b
48-49: Courtesy of Daniel Schwen
50-51: Used under license from iStockphoto.com
52-53: Anastassios Mentis / Alamy

54-55: Richard Levine / Alamy
56: Chris Batson / Alamy
60-61: Sandra Baker / Alamy
63: AP Photo/Diane Bondareff
64-65: Used under license from iStockphoto.com
66-67: AP Photo/Brian Branch-Price
68-69: AP Photo/Bloomberg for Mayor, Diane Bondareff
70: Courtesy of David Shankbone
72: AP Photo/Chao Soi Cheong
74-75: AP Photo/Beth A. Keiser, pool
75: Courtesy of Momos
76: AP Photo/James Estrin, Pool
78: AP Photo/Kathy Willens
78-79: AP Photo/Gregory Bull
82-83: Courtesy of Stephen Hilger
85: Used under license from iStockphoto.com
87: AP Photo/Jennifer Graylock
88: Courtesy of Michael Slonecker
92: Used under license from iStockphoto.com
92-93: AP Photo/James Keivom, Pool
94-95: AP Photo/Bryan Smith, Pool
98-99: AP Photo/Seth Wenig